The Concise
Lexicon
of
the
Occult

The Concise Lexicon of the Occult

by Gerina Dunwich

A Citadel Press Book
Published by Carol Publishing Group

Copyright © 1990 by Gerina Dunwich

A Citadel Press Book
Published by Carol Publishing Group

Editorial Offices
600 Madison Avenue
New York, NY 10022

Sales & Distribution Offices
120 Enterprise Avenue
Secaucus, NJ 07094

In Canada: Musson Book Company
A division of General Publishing Co. Limited
Don Mills, Ontario

Manufactured in the United States of America
10 9 8 7 6 5 4 3 2

Carol Publishing Group books are available at special discounts
for bulk purchases, for sales promotions, fund raising, or
educational purposes. Special editions can also be created to
specifications. For details contact: Special Sales Department,
Carol Publishing Group, 120 Enterprise Ave., Secaucus, NJ 07094

Library of Congress Cataloging-in-Publication Data

Dunwich, Gerina.
    The concise lexicon of the occult / by Gerina Dunwich.
      p. cm.
    "A Citadel Press book."
    ISBN 0-8065-1191-5 : $7.95
    1. Occultism--Dictionaries. I. Title.
  BF1407.D86   1990
  133'.03--dc20   90-41277
                                                           CIP

ABRACADABRA

A cabalistic word derived from the name Abraxas, a mighty Gnostic deity whose name means "hurt me not." The word Abracadabra, when chanted or when its letters are arranged in an inverted pyramid (a holy figure and symbol of trinity) and worn around the neck as a talisman for nine days, is said to possess the magickal power to ward off illness and to cure fever. At the end of that time, it is taken off and tossed over the shoulder into a stream flowing east. It is believed that the cool, rushing waters draw the heat of the fever away from the sick person and back to the rising sun, the source of all warmth.

ABRAMALIN MAGICK

A medieval practice of both white and black Ceremonial Magick involving spirit communication, word magick and palindromic magickal squares. Abramelin is a system based mainly on Hellenistic theurgy of the Iamblichan type, but with Jewish increments from the Qabbalah. Abramelin Magick sets forth the semi-Gnostic doctrine that the world was created and is maintained by demons (or Powers of Darkness) who work under the command of angelic spirits. With the proper purifications, tools, prayers and formulas, an Abramelin magician, with the help of angels, can control the demons of darkness and command them to do his or her will.

ABSENT HEALING

A form of faith healing involving the projection of positive healing energy to an ill person by a healer who is not present at the time of the healing.

ACUTO-MANZIA

The art and practice of divination using thirteen tacking pins. Ten straight pins and three bent pins are shaken together in a container and then dropped onto a lightly powdered table where their symbolic formations are interpreted.

ADEPT
One who has gained profound magickal powers and insights through initiation; an initiate or occult master.

ADLET
In Eskimo folklore, a race of cruel, blood-drinking monsters believed to be descended from a supernatural red dog.

ADORATION
In Voodoo, a Haitian Creole song which is performed after an animal is sacrificed to a loa, and at the end of the novena in the ritual cycle of the cult of the dead.

AELURANTHROPY
The zoomorphic ability to change from human to cat form by means of charms, magickal incantations or supernatural power. (See also ZOOMORPHISM)

AEROMANCY
The art and practice of divination from the sky and the air, extending beyond the range of weather prognostications and concentrating more upon spectral formations, shapes of clouds, comets and other phenomena of the heavens.

AFRITS
In Persian mythology and folk-legend, gigantic demons who inhabited dark caves and pits, and preyed on mortals with weapons of evil magick.

AFTERWORLD
The world of the dead; the place where human souls go to after death: a concept shared by all human mythologies and religions. The afterworld is usually perceived as a dark and gloomy underground region or as a bright and happy world in the sky.

AGENT
A man or woman who, in psychical research, transmits thoughts and psychic energies in telepathic experiments.

AGWE
A Rada Voodoo sea-god, patron loa of fishermen and sailors, and consort of the female loa Erzulie. Agwe is envisaged as a green-eyed half-caste often wearing the uniform of a naval officer.

AIR
One of the four alchemical elements. The spirits of Air are known as sylphs.

AIR SIGNS
The astrological signs attributed to the ancient element of Air are Aquarius, Gemini and Libra.

AIZAN
Haitian Voodoo loa who lives in water and gives his devotees the power to heal and divine the future.

AJATTARA
In Finnish folklore, a dragon-like female spirit who inhabits forests and is believed to suckle snakes and produce diseases. In southern Estonia, she is believed to be the Devil's daughter.

AKPOU
In Dahomean Voodoo, a slender iron rod dressed in a skirt and carried by travelers as a powerful magick charm to repel evil and protect them against ghosts.

ALASTOR
An evil, avenging spirit

ALCHEMIST
One who practices the ancient occult science of alchemy.

ALCHEMY
The ancient occult science of transmutation of base metals into gold or silver by both chemical and spiritual processes. The other major aims of alchemy were to find an elixir that could make humans immortal, and to acquire various methods of creating life artificially.

ALCHERA
In Australian Aboriginal mythology, the mythical past or "dream time" when totemic ancestral spirits lived and established the world and customs for their descendants to follow; also any object associated with the totem. (Also spelled alcheringa.)

ALECTRYOMANCY
A form of divination practiced mainly throughout Africa, whereby a bird (usually a black hen or a gamecock) is allowed to pick up grains of corn from a circle of letters to form names or words containing prophetic significance.

ALEUROMANCY
The art and practice of divination with flour. In ancient Greece, small pieces of paper containing messages were

rolled up in balls of flour, mixed up nine times, and then given to those who desired to know their destiny. This particular form of divination was ruled by the god Apollo The ancient practice of aleuromancy continues to be practiced in modern times in the form of fortune cookies

ALIMAGBA
A human-shaped carved figure worn as a magick charm by the Dahomey people to insure safety on a journey.

ALL HALLOW'S EVE
The Pagan festival and Witches' Sabbat of Samhain, celebrated on the last day of October. (For more information, see SAMHAIN.)

ALMADEL
A talisman fashioned in white wax, inscribed with the names of spirits or angels, and used in Ceremonial Magick rituals.

ALOMANCY
The art and practice of divining future events by interpreting the symbolic patterns made by sprinkling salt. The old superstition that spilling salt brings bad luck and that a pinch of salt sprinkled over the left shoulder averts the misfortune most likely stemmed from this ancient occult practice.

ALPHITOMANCY
The art and practice of divination to identify a guilty person by using a leaf of barley.

ALRAUN
In European folk magick, a small good-luck image shaped from the root of a mandrake or bryony.

AMBROSIA
In Roman and Greek mythology, the drink or food (nectar) of the gods which made immortal all humans who partook of it.

AMNIOMANCY
The art and practice of divination by observation of the caul on a child's head at the time of birth.

AMON
Ancient Egyptian god of life, reproduction and agriculture. He is represented as a man with a ram's head.

AMPHIPTERE
A legless, winged serpent which, according to legend, lived along the banks of the Nile and in Arabia. The amphiptere was a guardian dragon of frankincense bearing trees, and threatened all mortals who foolishly attempted to harvest the precious resin.

AMULET
A consecrated object (usually a small colored stone, or a piece of metal inscribed with runes or other magickal symbols) that possesses the power to protect a person or thing from threatening influences, evil and misfortune. Astrological jewelry, four-leaf clovers and a rabbit's foot are several examples of popular modern amulets.

ANAITIS
Persian goddess of fertility.

ANATHEMA
A Sorcerer's curse or an offering to a deity. It also is the word used in the Roman Catholic Church as part of the formula in the excommunication of heretics.

ANATHEMATIZE
To place a curse upon.

ANCHANCHU
In Aymara Indian folklore, a friendly-looking but evil demon who resides in rivers and isolated places, and sucks the blood of his human victims as they sleep.

ANGAKOK
A Central Eskimo shaman, medicine-man or magician who uses various sacred songs, invocations and incantations to cure the ill, control the weather, and drive away evil spirits from the village.

ANGELICA
A mystical plant associated with early Nordic magick. It was worn as a charm in the 15th century to protect against the dreaded plague. (According to folklore, an archangel revealed in a vision that the plant would cure the plague.) In many parts of the world, country peasants believed that angelica possessed the power to guard against evil, and they hung its leaves around their children's necks to protect them against the spells and enchantments of sorcerers. Angelica is both a culinary and a medicinal herb, and according to the 17th century herbalist Nicholas Culpepper, it should be gathered when the moon is in Leo.

ANHANGA
In Amazonian Indian folklore, a mischievous spirit or demon who inhabits forests and plays tricks on hunters and travelers.

ANJARA
In Hispanic folklore, a type of supernatural witch who appears in the guise of an elderly woman to test out the

charity of mortals. The anjara watches over animals and is believed to possess a golden staff which has the magickal power to transform everything it touches into riches.

ANIMISM
The spiritual belief that everything in nature, animate and inanimate, possesses an innate soul as well as a body.

ANKH
An ancient Egyptian symbol resembling a cross with a loop at the top. It symbolizes life and cosmic knowledge, and every major god and goddess of Egyptian mythology is depicted carrying it. Also known as the "crux ansata," it is used by many contemporary Witches in spells and rituals involving health, fertility and divination.

AN-SHET
A Witch's wand.

ANTHESTERIA
A three day long Greek festival held once a year in Athens in honor of the wine-god Dionysus.

ANTHROPOMANCY
An ancient and gruesome form of divination by interpreting the intestines of sacrificed children. This hideous method of divination was believed to have been practiced by the Emperor Julian the Apostate.

ANUBIS
Ancient Egyptian god of death and black magick who is envisaged as a dog or as a man with the head of a jackal. In Egyptian mythology, he was the son of Nephthys,

and at times he rivaled the great god Osiris in importance.

APANTOMANCY
The art and practice of drawing omens from chance meetings with animals or birds. (The old superstition of the black cat bringing bad luck when crossing a person's path is one example of apantomancy.)

APHRODITE
Greek goddess of love and beauty, and one of the Twelve Great Olympians. She is also known as Cytherea and is identified with the Roman love-goddess Venus.

APOLLO
Greek god of the sun, fertility, prophecy and oracles, and also a deity associated with light, healing, music and poetry. In Greek mythology, he was the son of Zeus, the twin brother of the lunar-goddess Artemis, and one of the Twelve Great Olympians.

APPARITION
The appearance of a person's phantom, living or dead, seen in a dream or in the waking state as the result of astral projection or clairvoyance.

APPORT
In spiritualism, a solid object that manifests during a seance by non-physical means.

AQUARIUS
In astrology, the eleventh sign of the zodiac, known as the Water-Bearer. Aquarius is an air sign, and is ruled by the planets Saturn and Uranus. The words unconventional, genius, dreamer, self-expressive, tempera-

mental, and out-going describe the typical Aquarian traits.

ARIES
In astrology, the first sign of the zodiac, symbolized by the ram. Aries is a fire sign, and is ruled by the planet Mars. Short-temperedness, intelligence, pride, impatience, extremism, courage, and self-centeredness are typical traits of persons born under the sign of Aries.

ARITHMANCY
The ancient art and practice of divination by numbers and letter values. Also known as arithmomancy, it was practiced mainly by the Greeks and Chaldeans, and is a precursor of numerology.

ARMOMANCY
The ancient art and practice of divination by observation of the shoulders of an animal that has been sacrificed.

ARRIANRHOD
Welsh Mother-Goddess and Neo-Pagan goddess of fertility.

ARTEMIS
Greek goddess of the moon, hunting and wild beasts As a lunar goddess, she has been an influential archetype for Witches and worshippers of the contemporary Goddess-religion. She is equivalent to the Roman moon-goddess Diana, and is identified with Luna, Hecate and Selene

ASAGWE
In Haitian Voodoo, a dance known as the "salute to the loas," characterized by sweeping circular movements, dips and semiprostations.

ASCENDANT
In astrology, the degree of the zodiac rising on the eastern horizon at the moment of an individual's birth; a rising sign.

ASHERALI
Canaanite goddess of the moon and fertility.

ASHIPU
Sorcerers and priests of ancient Babylonia who exorcised evil spirits, cured the ill, and performed rituals of magick to control nature and counteract evil spells.

ASPECT
In astrology, the number of degrees on an astrological chart between two planets.

ASPIDOMANCY
The art and practice of divination by sitting on a shield within a magick circle and falling into a trance while reciting ancient occult formulas.

ASPORT
In spiritualism, a solid object that disappears during a seance and often manifests elsewhere.

ASSON
In Voodoo, a sacred ceremonial rattle filled with seeds.

ASTARTE
Phoenician goddess of love and fertility. She is identified with the moon and is depicted with crescent horns.

ASTRAEA
Greek goddess of innocence and purity, daughter of Themis, and a deity associated with justice. It is said

that after leaving Earth, Astraea was placed among the stars where she became the constellation Virgo the Virgin.

ASTRAGLOMANCY
The art and practice of divination by dice. Also known as astragyromancy.

ASTRAL BODY
The double of the physical human body, but made of a much finer substance with a shining and luminous appearance. It is connected to the physical body by an etheric umbilical cord and is able to pass through solid obstructions and float about unhindered by gravity, space or time.

ASTRAL PLANE
The plane of existence and perception which parallels the dimension of the physical and is the plane that the astral body reaches during astral projection and death.

ASTRAL PROJECTION
An out of the body experience achieved by any number of trance-inducing methods or imagination techniques; the separation of the consciousness from the physical body resulting in an altered state of consciousness. Also known as astral travel.

ASTROLOGY
The science of the stars. An ancient occult art and science, dating back to the Third Century B.C., that judges the influence of the planets in the solar system upon the course of human affairs. In astrology, a planet's influence varies according to which section of the zodiac it is in. The two main types of astrology are: Mundane and

Horary. Mundane astrology, which is based on the premise that the Earth's physical structure is affected by cosmic influences, deals with the prediction of large-scale phenomena such as earthquakes, political trends and wars. Horary astrology is a method that uses charts for answering specific questions and/or solving problems. The other branches of astrology include: Electorial astrology, which calculates appropriate dates and times for undertaking important events such as marriage, travel, etc.; Inceptional astrology, which deals with the outcome of a particular event whose date, time and place have already been established; Medical astrology, which correlates zodiac signs and planetary influences with diseases and malfunctions of the bodily organs; Natal astrology, which focuses on the horoscope of the heavens for the precise moment of an individual's birth; Predictive astrology, which predicts future events in an individual's life; and Astrometeorology, which uses the science of the stars to forecast weather patterns and conditions.

ATHAME
A black-handled ritual knife with a double-edged blade, used by Witches to draw the circle and to store and direct energy during magickal rituals.

ATHENA
Greek goddess of wisdom and the arts. She is one of the Twelve Great Olympians and is identified with the Roman goddess Minerva.

ATTIS
Phrygian god of fertility and vegetation, and consort of the fertility-goddess Cybele.

AUGUR
(1.) A sign or omen. (2.) In ancient Rome, a magician-priest who studied the flight of birds to predict future events.

AUGURY
The ancient art and practice of divination by the flight of birds. Also the art, ability or practice of divination in general.

AUKI
In Peruvian Indian religion and folklore, a powerful mountain spirit who is called upon by sorcerers to help in divination and curing.

AURA
A colored light produced by heat energy and electromagnetic energy that emanates from the bodies of all living things; a psychic field of energy surrounding both animate and inanimate bodies.

AUREOLE
A circle of mystical light, similar to an aura, which is said to surround the head or body of a mystic, saint or deity; a halo.

AUSTROMANCY
The ancient occult art and practice of drawing omens from the winds.

AUTOMATIC WRITING
In spiritualism, a method of spirit communication by which a medium enters a dreamlike state of consciousness and allows a spirit guide to control his or her hand to write messages.

AUTOMATISM

In spiritualism and parapsychology, a general term for automatic writing, painting, drawing and speaking, performed by a spirit through a medium in trance.

AUTUMN EQUINOX SABBAT

The second festival of Harvest, and one of the foui Lesser Witches' Sabbats It is the time to celebrate the completion of the grain harvest which began at Lammas, and to pay homage to the Horned God. Many Wiccan traditions perform a special rite for the goddess Persephone's descent into the Underworld as part of their Autumn Equinox celebration.

AXIOMANCY

The ancient art and practice of divination by an axe or hatchet. Properly interpreted, the quivers of the axe handle, when driven into a post, are said to reveal the answers to questions. The way in which the axe handle falls to the ground is an old method used to point out the direction taken by a thief.

AYIDA WEDO

Haitian/Dahomean Voodoo loa envisaged as a rainbow-serpent of many colors. She is the consort of the serpent-loa Damballah, and is often symbolized by a snake, serpent or dragon.

AZIZA

In Dahomean folk belief, elf-like spirits of the forest known as the "little people", who give the power of magick and knowledge of the worship of the gods to humans.

BAAL
Phoenician god of nature and fertility, associated with winter rain. He is depicted as a warrior with a horned helmet and spear, and was once worshipped as the principal god on Earth for thousands of years.

BACCHANT
A priest, votary or male follower of the god Bacchus.

BACCHANTE
A priestess, votary or female follower of the god Bacchus. (plural: Bacchae)

BACCHUS
Roman god of wine and gaiety, identified with the Greek wine-god Dionysus. In mythology, he was the son of Zeus and Semele, and the consort of the goddess Ariadne. A drunken orgy-festival known as the Bacchanalia was celebrated in ancient Rome in honor of Bacchus. (Compare with ORGIA.)

BAJANG
In Malay folklore, a malignant spirit who takes the form of a polecat and whose presence presages disaster or illness. In certain areas of the Malay peninsula, the bajang is believed to be the enslaved spirit of a dead child, conjurable at midnight by special magickal incantations spoken over the grave.

BALIAN
Indonesian term for a spiritualist medium who communicates with spirits while in a trance-like state, conducts purification rituals, and divines the future.

BANISH
To release or drive away a conjured spirit from the power of the magick circle.

BANISHING RITUAL
In Ceremonial Magick, a ritual performed by a magician to remove negative or evil influences from the circle. In the banishing ritual of the Lesser Pentagram, a consecrated ceremonial sword is used to inscribe pentagrams in the air, archangels are invoked at the four quarters, and a special prayer known as the "Kabbalistic Cross" is recited.

BANSHEE
In Gaelic folklore, a female nature-spirit who takes the form of an old woman and presages a death in the family by wailing a mournful tune that sounds like the melancholy moaning of the wind. As a herald of death, the banshee is usually heard at night under the window of the person who is about to die.

BAPHOMET
A demonic god envisaged as a goat-headed creature with wings, the breasts of a woman and an illuminated torch between his horns. Also known as the mysterious "Bearded Demon," Baphomet was worshipped by inner circles of several occult brotherhoods and was identified with the Devil card of the Tarot by the 19th century magickal philosopher Eliphas Levi.

BAPTISM
Ritual immersion in water; any ceremony, trial or experience by which a woman or man is initiated, purified, or given a name.

BARGHEST
In folklore of Cornwall and northern England, a shrieking spirit who takes the form of a specter-hound or bear-ghost, and whose presence presages a death in the family.

BARON SAMEDI

In Voodoo, the Petro loa of death and black magick. He is the ruler of cemeteries and is envisaged as a black dwarf. His symbol is a black cross on a tomb, the cross draped with a black coat and surmounted with a top hat. He controls the souls of men and women murdered by evil sorcery, and it is said that when he is invoked at midnight, the bizarre and frightening sound of rattling chains is heard before he makes his appearance. Baron Samedi is the Petro loa most invoked in Voodoo black magick.

BARREN SIGNS

In astrology, the three signs of the zodiac which indicate a tendency toward barrenness: Gemini, Leo and Virgo.

BAST

Ancient Egyptian fertility-goddess and daughter of Isis, also known as the Lady of the Light. In ancient times, she was worshipped in the form of a cat. Later, She was envisaged as a woman with the head of a cat. Bast is one of the most popular ancient Egyptian goddesses in modern day Witchcraft and sex-magick cults.

BAU

Sumerian fertility goddess; the Great Mother and consort of Ningirsu. As a creatrix, she is identified with the serpent goddess Nintu and Gula the Healer.

BELL

A hollow, metallic instrument, usually cup-shaped with a flared opening, which emits a tone when struck by a clapper suspended within, or by a separate stick or hammer. Bells have been used by nearly all cultures throughout history as magickal talismans, fertility charms, summons to a deity, and as instruments for sacred music and religious rituals of widely varying beliefs. Many Witches and Wiccans use a consecrated bell as an altar tool to signal the beginning and/or close of a ritual or Sabbat. Vodun houngans and mambos of Haiti, as well as the tribal priests of Africa, use bells and dancing to invoke gods. Chinese magicians summon the rain and other forces of nature with special magickal bells, while Siberian shamans wear them for incantations and prophecies. Bells have also served as magickal or sacred tools to "ring out witches," exorcise demons and ghosts, protect animals and children from the power of the evil eye, to bless, and to divine the future.

BELOMANCY
The art and practice of divination by arrows. It was extensively practiced among the Chaldeans and Arabs. Three divining arrows marked with occult symbols, names or prophetic inscriptions would be cast into a quiver, mixed together, and then one would be drawn and interpreted. In certain countries, wands or small wooden sticks were used instead of arrows. (See RHABDOMANCY.)

BELTANE
One of the four Grand Witches' Sabbats, taking place on the first day of May, and known as May Day, May Eve, Rudemas, Rood Day, and Walpurgisnacht. The Beltane Sabbat is derived from an ancient Druid fire festival celebrating the union of the Goddess and the Horned God, and thus is also a fertility festival.

BESOM
A straw broom used by Witches in certain Wiccan ceremonies such as Handfasting and Candlemas. Although

the broom has always been associated with Witches, it was never actually used for flying. Instead, Witches practicing sympathetic magick would straddle the broom and jump up and down in order to show the crops how high to grow.

BEWITCHMENT
The act of gaining power or casting a spell over another person by means of Witchcraft or supernatural powers.

BIBLIOMANCY
The art and practice of divination by consultation of a randomly selected passage or line in a book, usually poetry or the Christian Bible.

BIGGHES
A set of ceremonial jewelry consisting of a leather garter, silver crown with crescent moon, bracelet and necklace worn by a Witch Queen or a High Priestess of a coven.

BIRTHSTONE
A jewel associated with a specific month or astrological sign of the zodiac. It is believed to attract good luck and repel negative or evil influences; however, it is unlucky to wear a stone of a month or sign other than one's own. Two exceptions, however, are jade and crystal, which are believed to bring good luck to all who wear or carry them as charms

BLACK ARTS
The practices of demonology and sorcery, a general term often extended to apply to the entire spectrum of occult subjects.

BLACK MAGICK
Negative magick performed with evil or selfish intent; any form of magick that signifies the destructive element, invokes malevolent forces, and is practiced to deliberately cause injury, misfortune or death to another person. Also known as sorcery.

BLACK MASS
In Satanism, a travesty of the Roman Catholic Mass in which sacred bread known as the host (representing the body of Jesus Christ in a Communion Service) is stolen from a church and desecrated. The Satanic Black Mass ceremony includes the backwards recitation of the Lord's Prayer and the alleged sacrifice of unbaptized children to the Devil.

BLETONISM
The art and practice of divination by drawing omens from currents of water.

BOANTHROPY
The zoomorphic ability to change from human to cow or bull by means of charms, magickal incantations or supernatural power. (See *Zoomorphism*.)

BOGGART
According to Yorkshire folklore, a mischievous spirit who appears in human form with the fur and tail of an animal.

BOKOR
A sorcerer who practices Voodoo black magick.

BOLLINE
A practical white-hilted working knife used by Witches to harvest sacred herbs, cut wands, slice bread and carve magickal symbols in candles and talismans.

BOMOR
A Malay medicine man who uses various forms of divination to determine the treatment of sick patients. The bomor also uses counter-charms, makes propitiatory offerings of food to the spirits, and brings back to the soul of the patient which is believed to be wandering in limbo whenever he or she is ill.

BONA DEA
Ancient Roman goddess of fertility and chastity, also known as Damia, Fatua, Oma, and identified with Cybele. Her annual festival was celebrated on the first day of May, and her worship was restricted to women. She is depicted as an elderly woman with pointed ears, holding a snake.

BOOBRIE
In Scottish Highland folklore, a supernatural waterbird which haunts lakes and salt wells.

BOOK OF CHANGES
The I Ching.

BOOK OF SHADOWS
A secret diary of magickal spells and potions kept by a Witch or a coven. In certain Wiccan traditions, a Witch's Book of Shadows must be burned in the event of his or her death in order to protect the secrets of the Craft.

BOTANOMANCY
The art and practice of divination by herbs or by burning branches of brier and vervain on which are inscribed questions to be answered.

BOUCAN
In Voodoo, a ritual bonfire lit prior to the New Year to symbolically re-fire the sun.

BRIGIT
Celtic and Neo-Pagan goddess of fire, wisdom, poetry and sacred wells, and also a deity associated with prophecy, divination and healing.

BRIZOMANCY
The art and practice of divination based on the prophetic inspiration of Brizo, a goddess of sleep.

BROOM GODDESS
In Chinese folk belief, a goddess named Sao Ch'ing Niang who is invoked in times of severe drought to send the rains.

BROWNIE
In English and Scottish Highland folklore, an elfin supernatural being in a brown hood and cloak who attaches himself to a family and does helpful work for them at night as they sleep, especially domestic chores.

BUNE WAND
An old Scottish nick-name given to the legendary Witches' broomstick, or any object supposedly used by Witches as a flying instrument.

BURIN
An engraving tool used by Witches and magicians to mark names or symbols ritually on athames, swords, bells and other magickal tools.

CABALA
See KABBALAH.

CAIRNS
Large stones or mounds of stones erected on the summits of hills, and used by the ancient Celtic Druids as sacrificial altars in the worship of their sun god.

CANCER
In astrology, the fourth sign of the zodiac, symbolized by the crab. Cancer is a water sign, and is ruled by the Moon. The name "Cancer" is Latin for "crab," and is derived from an ancient Greek myth about a crab who fought the Greek hero Hercules as he battled the monstrous Hydra. Moodiness, sensitivity, persistence, psychic awareness and an excellent memory are typical Cancerian traits.

CANDLE MAGICK
A form of sympathetic magick that uses colored candles to represent the people and things at which its spells are directed. Each color symbolizes a different attribute, influence and emotion. There are different astral colors for each of the twelve signs of the zodiac.

CANDLEMAS
One of the four Grand Witches' Sabbats, celebrated on February 2nd. Also known as Imbolc and Oimelc, it is a fire festival celebrating the Goddess of fertility and the Horned God. In ancient times, Candlemas was celebrated as the Feast of Pan.

CAPNOMANCY
The art and practice of divination through the study of smoke rising up from a fire, often associated with sacrificial offerings and incense thrown onto hot coals.

CAPRICORN
In astrology, the tenth sign of the zodiac, symbolized by the goat. Capricorn is an earth sign, and is ruled by the planet Saturn. Its name is Latin for "goat horn " Ambition, determination, faithfulness, materialism, pessimism and prudence are typical Capricornian traits

CARROMANCY
The art and practice of divination by the melting of wax to form symbolic patterns; divination by candles

CARTOMANCY
The art and practice of divination by cards, such as the Tarot, Gypsy Witch or Zenner cards.

CATOPTROMANCY
The art and practice of divination by means of a lens or magic mirror; an early form of scrying practiced by the ancient Greeks, using a mirror held in a fountain or turned to the moon to catch lunar rays.

CATOXTROMANCY
The art and practice of divination by looking glasses. See CATOPTROMANCY.

CATTABOMANCY
The art and practice of divination by vessels made of brass or other metal.

CAULDRON
In Witchcraft, a small, black cast iron pot that symbolically combines the influences of the four ancient elements. The cauldron represents the womb of the Goddess, and is used for various purposes including brewing potions, burning incense, and holding charcoal or herbs.

CAUSIMOMANCY
The art and practice of divination from objects placed in a fire. When an object cast into a fire did not burn, the omen was considered to be favorable.

CEARA
Ancient Pagan goddess of nature, and feminine equivalent to the god Cearas.

CEARAS
Ancient Pagan god of fire, and masculine equivalent to the goddess Cearas.

CELTIC CROSS
A Tarot card reading method.

CENSER
A fireproof incense burner used in magickal rituals and symbolic of the ancient element of Air.

CENTAUR
In mythology, a creature having the head, arms and trunk of a man, and the body and legs of a horse.

CENTEOTLE
Mexican goddess of fertility.

CEPHALOMANCY
The art and practice of divination from the broiled head or skull of an ass or goat.

CERAUNOSCOPY
The art and practice of divination by the interpretation of thunder and lightning.

CEREMONIAL MAGICK
The art and practice of controlling the powers of nature, which are conceived of as being either angelic or de-

monic, by conjuration of spirits with words of power or god-names. Ceremonial Magick employs elaborate rituals, dramatic invocations of spirits, and mystic sacraments.

CERES
Roman goddess of harvest and fertility, and the mother of Proserpina. In Greek mythology, she is called Demeter, and is the goddess of agriculture and the mother of Persephone.

CERNUNNOS
Celtic horned nature-god of wild animals, hunting and fertility, "Lord of All Living Creatures" and consort of the Great Mother. He is depicted as a hirsute man with antlers and hoofs, and his name literally means "The Horned One." In ancient times, he was worshipped in Britain and in Celtic Europe. As a Neo-Pagan god, he is worshipped mainly by Wiccans of the Gardnerian tradition.

CEROMANCY
The art and practice of divination by wax or lead. Warm, melted wax or molten lead is poured into cold water and the seer interprets the shapes that the wax or lead assumes, such as significant letters of the alphabet or symbolic patterns. Also known as ceroscopy and carromancy, this form of divination was common in Britain, Sweden and Lithuania.

CEROSCOPY
See CEROMANCY.

CERRIDWEN
Druidic lunar goddess and British goddess of mountains and fertility who brewed a Sacred Cauldron of Inspiration with herbs of magick.

CHAKRA
Any of the seven special points of psychic energy located within the human body that begins at the genital region and ends at the top of the skull.

CHALDEAN
A 17th century general term for a magician or a person versed in occult learning; an astrologer, soothsayer, or practitioner of the black art of sorcery. In ancient times, Chaldea (a region in southern Babylonia) was the center of magickal arts.

CHALICE
In Witchcraft, a sacred cup or goblet used to hold consecrated water or wine. The chalice symbolizes the ancient element of Water.

CHANEKOS
In Mexican and Central American folklore, a race of supernatural, dwarf-like creatures who steal the souls of humans, thus causing sickness or death.

CHANGELING
In Irish folklore, a fairy that secretly exchanges souls or identities with a newborn baby or a newly married woman.

CHARM
A highly magickal object that not only works like an amulet or talisman to counteract misfortune, but also can be used to bewitch others.

CHARTOMANCY
The art and practice of divination by writing in papers.

CHEIROGNOMY
The study of the shapes of hands and fingers and what they reveal about an individual's personality and physical health.

CHEIROMANCY
Palmistry or palm-reading; the study of the lines of the palm to disclose an individual's past and to predict their future. There are seven important lines on the palm of the hand and seven lesser ones. The important or main ones are: the line of Life, the line of Head, the line of Heart, the girdle of Venus, the line of Health, the line of the Sun, and the line of Destiny. The seven lesser ones are: the line of Mars, the Via Lasciva, the line of Intuition, the line of Marriage, and the three bracelet lines on the wrist.

CHICOMECOATL
Ancient Aztec goddess of nourishment whose name means literally "seven snakes". Her sacred symbol is an ear of corn as she is the female counterpart of Cinteotl, the god of maize. She is also known as Xilonen.

CHTHONIAN
See CHTHONIC.

CHTHONIC
Pertaining to the spirits and deities associated with the Underworld. The word chthonic, with a silent "ch", is pronounced as thonic (to rhyme with tonic).

CINGULUM
In Witchcraft, a consecrated cord (nine feet long and red) used by Witches when dancing to raise power. Nine knots on the cord are used for storing built-up power for future magickal use. To release the power,

the knots must be untied in the exact order in which they were tied.

CIRCUMAMBULATION
The ancient and wide-spread practice of walking around a person, object or site with the right hand towards it, either as a magickal rite, a religious ceremony, or an act of reverence. Also known as the "sunwise turn" and the "holy round," circumambulation has been performed by various cultures throughout history to bring good luck, cure diseases, bless the dead, wipe out sins, acquire magickal powers or transformation, and insure the continuation of the solar cycle.

CLAIRAUDIENCE
In spiritualism, an auditory form of ESP; the psychic ability to hear spirit voices and sounds attributed to the deceased.

CLAIRVOYANCE
In spiritualism, the extrasensory power to perceive objects or events that are out of the range of average human senses.

CLAIRVOYANT
In spiritualism, a person gifted with the power of clairvoyance.

CLEDONOMANCY
An ancient form of fortune-telling in which a dangling key is used to answer questions. See also DACTYLO-MANCY.

CLEROMANCY
The art and practice of divination by casting or drawing lots.

CLOC COSANCA
A flat, round, green stone with a hole in the middle. According to the ancient Celtic tradition, it offers good fortune and protects against evil when worn or carried as a charm.

CLURACAN
In Irish folklore, a fairy who inhabits wine cellars, and knows where secret treasure is hidden. It is said to appear as a dwarfish, aged man, and is often associated with the leprechaun.

COBLYNAU
See WICHTLEIN

COCO MACAQUE
In Haitian Voodoo, a magickal stick that walks by itself and is believed to possess the supernatural power to kill enemies.

COLLAHUAYA
Hereditary herbalists and practitioners of magick in the Bolivian provinces of Caupolican and Munecas.

COMUS
Roman god of revelry, drunkenness and mirth. He is depicted as a winged youth crowned with roses, dressed in white and bearing a torch.

CONCORDIA
Roman goddess of peace and harmony, whose symbols are the herald's staff entwined by serpents and two

clasped hands. She is identified with the Greek goddesses Aphrodite, Pandemos and Harmonia. Concordia
is depicted as a matronly figure holding an olive branch
in her right hand and the cornucopia in her left.

CONE OF POWER
In Witchcraft, the ritual act of visualizing energy in the
form of a spiral light rising from the magick circle and
directing it towards a specific goal or task.

CONGA
In Haitian Voodoo, a category of loas associated with
the Rada group in the organization of the Vodun
pantheon.

CONJUNCTION
In astrology, the situation when two planets are within
five degrees of each other.

CONJURATION
In ceremonial magick, the act of evoking spirits by
means of formulas or words of power.

CONSECRATION
The act, process or ceremony of making something sacred; the ritual use of water and salt to exorcise negative
energies and/or evil influences from ritual tools, the
magick circle, etc.

CONSUS
Ancient Roman god of stored harvest, good counsel,
secret deliberations and the underworld. The two sa-

cred festivals of Consus (the Consualia) were held yearly on the 21st of August and the 15th of December.

CONTACT HEALING
Spiritual healing by means of laying-on-of-hands. See PRANA.

CONTACT TELEPATHY
In parapsychology, the paranormal ability to read another person's mind through physical contact and intense concentration. See also TELEPATHY.

CONTROL
In spiritualism, a spirit-guide that presents itself through a medium in trance, usually on a regular basis, and acts as an intermediary with other spirits who wish to communicate with the living.

COPAL
A sacred incense made from the gum secreted from the trees of the genus Elaphrium. Copal was used by native Middle Americans in pre-conquest times, and is widely used today in many Christian and Neo-Pagan ceremonies.

CORN DOLLY
In Witchcraft and folk-legend, a human or animal figure fashioned from the last sheaf of corn from a harvest and used in Lammas and Autumn Equinox Sabbots as a sacred symbol of the Goddess and the fertility of the Earth. In England, Germany and Scotland, the corn

dolly is kept to ensure a bountiful harvest for the following year.

CORRIGAN
In Brittany folklore, a female fairy who steals human children and leaves a changeling in their place She is believed to have been an ancient Druidess.

COSCINOMANCY
The art and practice of divination by sieves.

COUNTERCHARM
In Witchcraft, a powerful magickal charm that is used to either neutralize or reverse the effects of another charm or spell.

COUNTERSPELL
In Witchcraft, a powerful magickal spell or incantation that neutralizes or reverses the effects of another spell or charm.

COVEN
In Witchcraft, a group of Witches, lead by a Priestess and/or a Priest, who gathers together to work magick and perform ceremonies at Sabbats and esbats.

COVENER
A man or woman who is a member of a coven.

COVENSTEAD
The place where a coven meets.

COWAN
Among Witches, a person who is not a Witch.

THE CRAFT
Witchcraft, Wicca, the Old Religion, the practice of folk magick.

CRITHOMANCY
The art and practice of divination by grain or corn (similar to critomancy).

CRITOMANCY
The art and practice of divination by interpreting omens drawn from barley cakes

CROMNIOMANCY
The art and practice of divination by interpreting omens drawn from onion sprouts.

CRYPTESTHESIA
A general term of psychic perception, coined by Dr. Charles Richet (1850–1935), a Nobel prize-winning physiologist and prominent researcher of psychic phenomena.

CRYSTAL BALL
A ball of crystal or glass used for scrying. The crystal ball is the focus for the scryer's psychic perception and does not, in itself, cause the visions to materialize.

CRYSTAL-GAZING
See SCRYING.

CRYSTALOMANCY
The art and practice of divination by gazing into a crystal ball or mirror-like pool of water; crystal-gazing; scrying.

CUBOMANCY
The art and practice of divination by thimbles.

CUPID
Roman god of love who was depicted as a winged boy
with five arrows and a bow. He is identified with the
Greek god Eros.

CUPS
One of the four suits of the Minor Arcana of the Tarot,
ascribed to the element of Water.

CURSE
In black magick and sorcery, a deliberate concentration
of destructive negative energy, often accompanied by
the invocation of evil spirits or demons, and intended to
harm a particular person, thing or place.

CURUPIRA
In Brazilian tribal mythology, a small demon who inhabits forests and is the protector of wild animals.

CUSP
In astrology, the transitional first or last part of a house
or sign of the zodiac. A person born on a cusp (between
two signs) is said to possess both the positive and negative traits of both signs.

CYBELE
Phrygian goddess of nature and fertility, consort of the
god Attis, and equivalent to the Greek goddess Rhea.
Cybele is symbolically associated with wild animals and
mountains, and is represented in myth riding in a chariot drawn by lions.

CYCLOMANCY
The art and practice of divination by a turning wheel

CYNANTHROPY
The zoomorphic ability to assume the physical form and characteristics of a dog by means of charms, magickal incantations or supernatural power. See ZOOMOR-PHISM.

DACTYLOMANCY
The art and practice of divination by rings; an early form of radiesthesia with a dangling ring (usually a wedding ring) used as a pendulum to indicate numbers and/or words by its swinging motion.

DAGHDA
Principal god of the Pagan tribes of Ireland, Lord of Great Knowledge, and god of fertility and the Earth. He was believed to control life and death with a great club and had a cauldron with magickal powers.

DAMBALLAH
In Voodoo, a powerful loa known as the Serpent of the Sky, Father of the Falling Waters, and loa of all spiritual wisdom. Damballah is the consort of Ayido Wedo and is worshipped and invoked on his sacred day Thursday.

DAPHNOMANCY
The art and practice of divination by interpreting the crackling of laurel branches thrown into an open fire.

DEICIDE
The act of murdering or killing a divine being, such as the crucification of Jesus Christ.

DEIFICATION
The transformation of a mortal being into a god or goddess.

DEIFY
To worship or revere as a god or goddess.

DEITY
A supreme or divine being; a god or goddess.

DEJA VU
The feeling of having previously experienced some-thing actually being experienced for the first time. Deja vu is regarded to be evidence of reincarnation.

DEMETER
Greek goddess of fertility, husbandry and harvest, and an important deity in the mysteries of the Eleusis. In mythology, Demeter is the mother of Persephone and is identified with the Roman goddess Ceres.

DEMIGOD
The semi-divine offspring of a mortal and a deity.

DEMONIAC
One who is possessed or thought to be possessed by a demon or evil spirit.

DEMONIC POSSESSION
A condition whereby a person's physical body is in-vaded and taken over by negative forces or demonic spirits who cause the sufferer to behave in bizarre, frightening or dangerous ways.

DEMONOLOGY
The study of demons and evil spirits, and the rituals and folk-legends associated with them.

DEMONOMANCY
The art and practice of divination through the evocation of demons.

DEO
In Hinduism, any one of the thirty-three great divine beings. Also known as devas.

DEOSIL
A Wiccan word meaning clockwise. In spells and rituals, deosil movement symbolizes life and positive energy.

DESTINY
The inevitable or necessary fate to which one is destined.

DEVIL
See SATAN.

DEVIL-WORSHIP
Satanism.

DEW
Greek goddess of fertility.

DIANA
Roman and Neo-Pagan lunar goddess and Mother-Goddess. She is identified with the Greek lunar goddess Artemis, and worshipped mainly by Wiccans of the Dianic tradition.

DIANIC
A Wiccan tradition or type of coven that worships only the Goddess or accords the Horned God secondary status to the Goddess. Dianic feminist Wicca encourages female leadership and involves its practitioners in many feminist issues. Although some covens of the Dianic tradition include both female and male members, many of them exclude men, and some are Lesbian-oriented.

DIDI
In Dahomean Voodoo, a magick charm containing a piece of lion's skin which is used by hunters to protect

themselves against lion attacks and impart a lion's strength to the wearer of the charm.

DIONYSUS
Greek god of wine, ecstasy, nature and fertility who was worshipped in frenzied orgies. He symbolizes freedom and spontaneous impulses, and is the equivalent of the Roman wine-god Bacchus.

DIRECT VOICE
In spiritualism, a phenomenon whereby a spirit speaks through a medium in trance during a seance.

DIRECT WRITING
In spiritualism, messages written by spirits without the agency of mediums or other living persons.

DISSOCIATION
A term used to describe an astral projection.

DIVINATION
The occult science, art and practice of discovering the unknown and foretelling events of the future by interpreting omens or by various methods of divination such as Tarot cards, dice, crystal balls, Ouija boards, astrology, etc.

DIVINING ROD
A forked stick or branch used to find subterranean water or hidden buried treasure by bending downward when held over the source.

DIVINITY
A god or goddess.

DIVINIZE
To worship or regard as a god or goddess.

DJINNI
See JINNI.

DOMOVIK
In Russian folk belief, a household spirit who watches over and protects the inhabitants of the house.

DOPPELGANGER
The human double, astral body or ghost resembling a living person. The word is derived from a German expression meaning Double Walker. A doppelganger is visible to the person it resembles and can also appear to others as an apparition.

DOUBLE
An astral body or doppelganger.

DOWSE
To use a divining rod.

DOWSER
One who uses a divining rod.

DRAC
In French country folklore, an enormous flesh-eating dragon that enchants and lures its mortal victims, usually women, into rivers and traps them there. The Drac is also believed to be an ancient creature, wise in sorceries, who feeds its own hatchlings with the milk of mortal women.

DRAGON
In various mythologies and folk-legends, a fire-breathing creature represented as a gigantic reptile having a lion's claws, the tail of a serpent, wings and scaly skin.

DRILBU

In Tibetan religion, a sacred prayer-bell rung by the lamas to attract good spirits and scare away evil ones.

DRUIDS

Priests of pre-Christian religion among the ancient Celtic nations in Gaul, Britain and Germany; believed by some to be either colonists from the fabled continent of Atlantis or descendants of Atlantean priests. The three classes of Druids that existed were the Prophets, the Priests, and the Bards. The Druids identified their supreme god 'Be'al" with the sun, worshipped in sacred groves, and also prayed to numerous inferior deities. They performed both animal and human sacrifices to their gods, and observed two festivals each year: Beltane ("fire of God"), which took place on the first day in May, and Samhain ("fire of peace"), which was held on October 31st and celebrated as the ancient Celtic New Year. The Druids performed the functions of priests, religious teachers, judges, and civil administrators, and were skilled in the arts of magick, astrology and herbalism. They also believed that the soul was immortal and continuously renewed itself by passing into the physical body of a newborn baby upon the death of an individual. The oak tree and the mistletoe (known as the "Golden Bough") were sacred to the Druids and regarded as being highly magickal. On the sixth day of the full moon, Druid priests, garbed in flowing white robes, carefully harvested the mistletoe with a golden sickle and used it in healing rituals and fertility rites. Druidism flourished from the 2nd century B.C. until the Roman conquest in the 2nd century A.D.; however, in many parts of Ireland and Scotland, Druidism continued until the coming of the Christian missionaries many centuries later. After many Druids were converted to Christianity, the old Celtic religion disappeared.

DURGA

Hindu goddess and consort of the god Shiva who was worshipped throughout India, especially in Bengal. Durga is represented as a ferocious ten-armed dragon-slayer, but it is said that she is loving and gentle to those who worship her.

DZOKHK

In Armenian mythology, a hell-like abyss beneath the earth where sinful souls are tortured by devils and demons with red-hot iron staffs.

EARTH
One of the four alchemical elements. The spirits of the element Earth are known as gnomes.

EARTH SIGNS
In astrology, the three signs of the zodiac attributed to the element of Earth: Capricorn, Taurus and Virgo.

ECTOPLASM
In spiritualism, a mysterious white substance which is said to emanate from the bodies or mouths of spiritualist mediums in trance during a seance.

EIDOLISM
The belief in disembodied spirits, ghosts and souls.

EIDOLON
A phantom, apparition, human double or astral body.

EKEKO
An ancient fertility spirit of the Aymara Indians who brings good luck to his worshipers. Ekeko's sacred feast, the Alasita, was celebrated on the solstice of summer.

EKE-NAME
In Witchcraft and Wicca, a Witch's secret name, also known as a Witch-Name. Many Witches take on one or more secret names to signify their rebirth and new life within the Craft. Eke-names are most sacred and are used only among brothers and sisters of the same path. When a Witch takes on a new name, he or she must be careful to choose one that harmonizes in one way or another with numerological name-numbers, birth-numbers, or runic numbers. A well-chosen name vibrates with that individual and directly links him or her to the Craft.

ELEMENTALS
In Witchcraft and magick, spirit-creatures that personify the qualities of the four ancient elements of Fire, Water, Air and Earth. Salamanders are the elemental spirits of Fire; Undines are the elemental spirits of Water; Sylphs are the elemental spirits of Air; Gnomes are the elemental spirits of Earth.

ELEMENTAL SIGNS
The signs of Fire, Water, Air and Earth. Fire is the symbol of energy, individuality and identity; Water is the symbol of life and spirit; Air is the symbol of the mind; Earth is the symbol of strength, fertility and the emotions.

ELF
In folklore, a small, fairy-like creature who inhabits gardens and woods, and is said to be mischievous.

ELLE WOMAN
In Danish folk belief, the spirit of the elder tree.

EMMA
In Japanese Buddhism, the rulers of the underworld.

ENCHANTMENT
Magick; the act of bewitching or casting a spell upon.

ENTITY
In spiritualism, a disembodied spirit, ghost or apparition.

ENVOUTEMENT
In Voodoo, a type of homeopathic or sympathetic magick which involves the use of special dolls to represent

the man or woman whom the healing or harmful power of a spell is directed at.

EOS
In Greek mythology, the winged goddess of dawn. She is identified with the Roman goddess Aurora.

EOSTRE
Saxon and Neo-Pagan goddess of fertility and spring-time whom the holiday of Easter was originally named after.

EPONA
Celtic mare-goddess.

ERESHKIGAL
Sumerian horned-goddess and Queen of the Under-world. She is identified with the Greek lunar-goddess Hecate, and is depicted as having the body of a fish with serpent-like scales and the ears of a sheep.

EROS
Greek god of love and sexual intercourse, the son of Zeus and Aphrodite, and the personification of univer-sal passion. He is identified with Cupid, the Roman god of love and the son of Venus.

ERZULIE
In Voodoo, the Rada loa of love, beauty and femininity. Her primary attribute is luxury and she is envisaged as a young, beautiful, wealthy lady wearing many golden rings and necklaces. Her favorite drink is champagne and, like the Virgin Mary, her symbol is a pierced heart. But unlike the Virgin Mary, Erzulie possesses a highly erotic character. She is the consort of both Agwe and Ogoun. In her Petro form, she is called Erzulie Ge-

Rouge (Erzulie Red Eyes) and is envisaged as a pale, trembling woman who sobs uncontrollably because no one can love her enough. White and pink are her sacred colors and her sacred day of the week is Friday.

ESBAT
In Witchcraft, a regular meeting of a Witches' coven that is held during the full moon at least thirteen times a year. At an esbat, the coveners exchange ideas, discuss problems, perform special rites, work magick and healing, and give thanks and/or request help from the Goddess and Horned God.

ESMERALDA
South American goddess of love.

E.S.P.
Extrasensory Perception.

EVIL EYE
In folk-legend and sorcery, the inborn supernatural power to cause bewitchment, harm, misfortune or death to others by an angry or venomous glance.

EVOCATION
In Ceremonial Magick, the summoning of a spirit or other non-physical entity using spells or words of power.

EXORCISM
The expulsion of an evil spirit, demon or Satanic force from a possessed person or place by a command, ritual or special prayer.

EXTERIORIZATION
Astral projection.

EYE OF HORUS

An ancient Egyptian symbol which depicts the divine
eye of the god Horus, represents both solar and lunar
energies, and is often used in contemporary Witchcraft
as a symbol of spiritual protection as well as the clairvoyant power of the Third Eye.

FAERIE
See FAIRY.

FAET FIADA
A powerful magickal spell used by the ancient Druids to either make themselves invisible or to enable them to see others who were. The faet fiada was also used to transform men into animals.

FAIRY
In folklore, tiny supernatural creatures in human form possessing magickal powers and bringing either good or bad luck to people through their spells and enchantments.

FAKIR
A Hindu mystic who performs feats of magic and endurance such as snake-charming, walking on hot coals and sitting on beds of nails without feeling pain.

FAMILIAR
In medieval Witchcraft and folklore, an attendant spirit that appears in the form of a cat, lizard, hare, toad or other small animal to aid a Witch in the practice of magick. According to legend, every time the familiar performs a service, the Witch must prick her finger and feed it a drop of her blood.

FASCINATION
The act of using the evil eye to mesmerize victims so that one can cause ill health to befall them.

FAUN
In Roman mythology, nature deities or supernatural creatures represented as having the body of a human and the horns, ears, tail and legs of a goat.

FAUNUS
Roman god of nature, woodlands and fertility. He is depicted as half-goat and half-human, and was worshipped mainly by farmers and shepherds.

FAUSTIAN MAGICK
The evocation of demons.

FETCH
In folklore, the ghostly apparition or double of a living person which was believed to be an omen of that person's death; a Witch's astral body.

FETCH-LIGHT
In English and Irish folklore, a supernatural light resembling the flame of a candle. It is believed to be an omen of death for those who see it. (Also called a fetch-candle.)

FETISH
A symbolic material object or talisman believed among primitive cultures to possess the magickal or supernatural power to protect and ward off evil.

FETISHISM
The belief in and worship of fetishes.

FIRE
One of the four alchemical elements. The spirits of Fire are known as Salamanders.

FIREDRAKE
In Celtic and Germanic folklore, a ferocious fire-breathing dragon which inhabits caves and guards hidden treasure

FIRE OF AZRAEL
A scrying fire

FIRE SCRYING
A form of divination by interpretation of symbolic visions of the past, present or future received while scrying (gazing) into flames or burning embers.

FIRE SIGNS
In astrology, the signs of the zodiac attributed to the ancient element of Fire: Aries, Leo and Sagittarius.

FIRESTICK
A Witch's wand.

FLAGAE
Familiar-spirits that appear in mirrors and reveal obscure information or esoteric truths to Witches and magicians.

FLAGELLATION
The art or practice of ritual scourging.

FLYING OINTMENT
In medieval Witchcraft, an ointment containing fat and various hallucinogenic herbs such as henbane, belladonna and mandrake. The flying ointment was rubbed on the body to enable a Witch to fly through the air on a broomstick.

FLYING SAUCER
An Unidentified Flying Object.

FORECAST
A psychic or astrological prediction concerning future events; to predict the future by means of astrology, dreams or clairvoyance.

FORTUNA
Roman goddess of happiness, good fortune and chance who was said to possess the power to bestow upon

mortals either wealth or poverty. She is identified with the Greek goddess Tyche.

FORTUNE-TELLER
One who predicts future events in a person's life through various forms of divination such as palmistry, numerology, Tarot cards, etc.

FRAVASHI
An occult love-priestess or Sufi sacred harlot (also known as the "spirit of the way") trained to teach sexual mysticism.

FREY
Scandinavian god of fertility, who is appropriately represented with an erect phallus indicating his fertilizing power. He is also a deity associated with peace and prosperity. In Scandinavian mythology, he is the brother and consort of the goddess Freya, and the son of the sea-god Njord.

FREYA
Scandinavian goddess of fertility, love and beauty, whose sacred symbols and familiars were cats. She is represented in myth as a beautiful woman riding in a golden chariot drawn by cats. She was also a queen of the Underworld and the sister and consort of the god Frey. As a Neo-Pagan goddess, she is worshipped mainly by Wiccans of the Saxon tradition.

FRIGGA
Scandinavian Mother-Goddess and consort of the god Odin. She was also the patroness of marriage and fecundity, and is represented in myth riding in a chariot drawn by sacred rams.

FRIJA
Pagan-Germanic Earth-Mother and consort of the god Tiwaz.

FUATH
In Scottish folklore, an evil water-spirit with yellow hair, webbed feet, a tail and a mane.

FUDO
Japanese god of wisdom.

FUTHORC
The name of the "alphabet" of the runes, and an acronym of the first six runic characters of the Anglo-Saxon (or Celtic) system: Feoh, Ur, Thorn, Os, Rad, Cen.

FYLFOT CROSS
In Ceremonial Magick, an ornamental symbol resembling a swastika which is divided into squares bearing the twelve signs of the zodiac and the four signs of the ancient alchemical elements with a solar symbol in the center.

FYLGJA
In Norwegian folklore, a tutelary spirit regarded as either a person's double which is conceived of in animal form, a guardian spirit which appears in dreams to give advice or warning, or as a person's soul which passes to another member of the family after death. According to folk belief, it is considered an omen of death to see one's own fylgja, except in a dream.

GAD
Semetic god of fortune

GAEA
Greek goddess of earth and fertility whose cult was wide-spread in ancient Greece. She is the personification of the earth, and in Rome she was worshipped as the goddess Terra. In mythology, she was the consort of Uranus and mother of the Titans, the Furies, and the Cyclopes

GANCONER
In Irish folklore, a debonair, pipe-smoking elf who seduces young mortal women that venture alone into the wild. It is said that the Ganconer (whose name means literally "Love Talker") always disappeared after his romantic interludes, leaving his mortal lovers to pine and die.

GANESHA
In Hindu mythology and religion, the god of wisdom, prudence, and learning. He is depicted in Saivite shrines as a red or yellow, pot-bellied man having four hands and the single-tusked head of an elephant, which symbolizes his power to remove obstacles.

GA-OH
In Seneca (Iroquois) Indian mythology, a benevolent spirit who lives in the sky and controls the four winds and the seasons.

GARTERS
In Wicca, long laces or strings that are tied around the leg above the knee and regarded as a sign of rank among Witches.

GASTROMANCY
The art and practice of divination by means of ventriloquism, or by the sounds of or signs upon the belly.

GEKKA-O
Japanese god of marriage

GELLER EFFECT
The paranormal ability to bend metal objects through the power of the mind.

GELOSCOPY
The art and practice of divination by interpretation of a person's laughter.

GEMINI
In astrology, the third sign of the zodiac, also known as the sign of the Twins. Gemini is an air sign, and is ruled by the planet Mercury. Charm, curiosity, eloquence, fickleness, generosity and restlessness are typical traits of persons born under the sign of Gemini.

GENETHLIALOGY
The astrological science, art and practice of calculating future events and studying personal characteristics from the influence of the stars at the moment of a person's birth.

GENIE
See JINNI.

GENIOS
Witches' familiars in Peruvian Witchcraft and magick.

GEOMANCY
The art and practice of divination by dropping objects (such as small stones, sticks, seeds) on the ground and then interpreting their patterns.

GHEDE
In Voodoo, the loa of death. Ghede is the loa invoked at the close of every Rada ceremony. He is said to dress in the colorful attire of a clown or court jester, and often wears between his legs a giant wooden phallus, sings dirty songs in a nasal voice and delights in embarrassing people in a sexual way. At Great Ceremonies, black goats and chickens are sacrificed to him as offerings. Ghede is known to have an insatiable hunger, and a person under his possession will eat prodigious amounts of ritual food offered. His sacred day is Saturday and black is his favorite color. Although Ghede is the loa of death, he can also be a great healer. In his Petro form, he is known as Baron Samedi, the Ruler of Cemeteries.

GHOST
The spirit or apparition of a dead person that returns to haunt living persons or former habitats; the disembodied astral body of a man or woman who has died. Also known as a phantom, shade, specter, and wraith.

GHOUL
In Moslem folklore, an evil spirit or demon that plunders graves and eats the flesh of human corpses.

GIANT
In various folk legends and myths, an enormous supernatural being possessing either human, animal or bird form, sometimes able to shift size and shape. Giants were also portrayed as barbaric, shaggy monsters of extraordinary size, often given to evil deeds. In the legends of ancient Greece, giants were said to be great human-like creatures with the tails of dragons who dwelled in fiery, volcanic regions.

GIANTESS
In various folk-legends and myths, a female giant. (See GIANT)

GLYPH
A powerful magickal symbol representing the name and date of birth of a person, and often worn as a charm to protect against bad luck or disease.

GNOMES
Elemental spirits of the Earth; in folklore, mischievous and ugly dwarf-like creatures associated with buried treasures and believed to inhabit underground regions. Also known as elves and goblins.

GOBLINS
See GNOMES.

GOLEM
In medieval Jewish folk-legend, a soulless human figure molded out of clay or virgin soil, and brought to life by men schooled in texts. It was said that rabbis animated the golems by walking clockwise around them while reciting magickal formulas consisting of a powerful combination of Hebrew letters, and the secret name of God. Other methods of bringing the golem to life were to inscribe its forehead with the Hebrew name for "truth" (*emet*), or to slip a piece of parchment inscribed with a magickal formula under the tongue of the golem, or into a slit in its head. To change the golem into a formless, lifeless mound of clay, all one had to do was remove the parchment. (However, according to legend, the golem returns every thirty-three years even after it has been destroyed.) Golems did not possess the ability to speak, but they were useful as servants, builders and errand boys. They were also used to guard and protect

against enemies, gather secret information, light fires and perform duties not permissible to Jews on the Sabbath. Like other magickal creatures, golems possessed a willful streak, and their ever-increasing size made them a threat to the very people they were summoned to serve.

GRAPHOLOGY

The art and practice of character analysis from handwriting; handwriting-analysis. In graphology, details of the breadth and height of each letter, the degree of slant, space between lines, letters and words, and general presentation are taken into consideration. In the year 1622, the first treatise on the subject of handwriting analysis appeared, and in the late 19th century, efforts at graphological systemization began with the work of the French abbe Hypolite Michon (1806–81). The science of graphology (which is often regarded as an occult science although it is never used in a predictive capacity) is divided into two schools of thought: Gestalt and Trait-stroke. The Gestalt theory teaches that a complete personality picture is made by the movement, form, and arrangement of handwriting, and that it must be analyzed altogether. The Trait-stroke theory teaches that each individual stroke possesses a different meaning. Theoretically, the page symbolizes the world, and the handwriting (which consists of over twenty elements) symbolizes the different, yet interrelated, aspects of the writer's personality, and his or her relationship with the world. Handwriting, which is a direct projection from the brain, is said to accurately reveal people's true feelings about themselves, what motivates them, how they react to any given situation, whether or not they are likely to realize their goals, etc. Many graphologists use a unique method of handwriting analysis which divides each letter of the alphabet into three parts (upper, middle and lower) to reveal the writer's physical and sexual qualities, emotions, and spirituality.

GREMLIN
A mischievous demon, imp or supernatural being who causes mechanical problems in military aircrafts.

GRIFFIN (also GRYPHON)
In Greek mythology, a feathered beast with the head and wings of an eagle and the body and legs of a lion. They were believed to be the guardians of the sun and were sacred to the god Apollo. Griffins lived on the tops of mountains, built their nests out of gold, and laid agates instead of eggs.

GRIMOIRE
A magickal workbook containing spells, formulas, rituals and incantations; any collection of magickal spells and formulas.

GRIS-GRIS
In Voodoo, a powerful charm prepared at the time of a full moon and filled with various offerings to a loa; a witch-doctor who sends forth evil spells and bewitchments.

GRYPHON
See GRIFFIN.

GUIDE
In spiritualism, a guardian spirit that offers advice and guidance through a spiritualist medium in trance during a seance.

GUIVRE
In folk-legend and mythology, a legless, wingless serpent with the horned and bearded head of a dragon. The guivres were dangerous creatures which were believed to inhabit forests and wells.

GULA
Babylonian goddess of healing and creativity; the consort of Ningrisu, and a deity associated with Shamash invocations.

GURU
A spiritual leader or teacher.

GYPSY
One of a nomadic Caucasoid people believed to be of Indian origin and traditionally associated with palmistry and Tarot card divination.

GYROMANCY
The art and practice of divination by rounds or circles.

HACHIMAN
Japanese god of war.

HADES
Greek god of the Underworld, ruler of the dead, and brother of the mighty god Zeus. Also known as Aidoneus, in Roman mythology he is called Pluto.

HAFERBOCK
In German folklore, a spirit who inhabits fields, and whose name means literally "the oat goat."

HAG
In various folklore, an evil sorceress or she-demon believed to be in league with the Devil or the dead. She is portrayed as an old woman with a hideous appearance.

HAGGING
The act of projecting the astral body or "changing the skin" by means of singing a special charm song, according to the magicians of the West Indies.

HALKA
The Sufi word for the magick circle of worship in which dancing, chanting, and other ritual activities are performed.

HALLOWEEN
See SAMHAIN.

HALOMANCY
See ALOMANCY.

HAMADRYAD
In Greek and Roman mythology, one of a group of

wood nymphs who inhabits oak trees and lives only as long as the tree of which she is the spirit.

HANDFASTING

In Wicca, a beautiful ceremony that joins a man and a woman "for as long as love shall last" and allows them to freely go their separate ways should they ever fall out of love with each other. Handfasting is usually performed during the waxing moon by a priestess and/or priest of a coven. White robes and flowers are normally worn by all attending the ceremony, although some covens prefer to work skyclad. Rings of gold or silver with the names of the bride and groom inscribed on them in runes are traditionally exchanged in addition to the vows of love.

HAND OF GLORY

In Medieval sorcery, a gruesome charm made from the mummified hand of a hanged criminal. It was used mainly by thieves as a magickal tool to paralyze or put their victims to sleep so that they could easily rob them. The Hand of Glory was an extremely popular element in evil spells and is one of the most famous charms in the history of black magick. To make a Hand of Glory, according to an ancient grimoire of magick and sorcery, the severed hand of a gibbeted felon must be wrapped in a piece of burial shroud, squeezed tightly to remove any remaining blood, pickled in an earthenware pot with salt, saltpeter and long peppers for two weeks, and then dried in full sunlight or in an oven with vervain and fern. A candle made from virgin wax, Lapland sesame and the fat from the hanged man is then placed in the hand, and as long as the flame of the candle burns, the power of the charm will work. According to legend, the only way to protect oneself against the

Hand of Glory and to render the charm powerless is to extinguish the candle flame by dowsing it with milk.

HANDPARTING
In Wicca, a ceremony that dissolves the marriage partnership of a man and a woman.

HANUMAN
In Hindu mythology and religion, the sacred monkey god worshipped by wrestlers and women who desired children. He is depicted in art as a yellow-skinned monkey with an endless tail.

HARPY
In Greek mythology, a hideous creature having the head and trunk of a woman and the wings, talons and tail of a vulture. The harpies controlled the storm winds and were said to be voracious monsters.

HARVEST DOLL
A doll made from the last sheaf of the harvest and regarded as the embodiment of the spirit of the crops. Also called a "corn dolly" and a "kern baby".

HATHA YOGA
The practice of physical postures and breathing exercises to attain spiritual integration.

HATHOR
Ancient Egyptian goddess of love, beauty and the heavens, and patroness of fecundity, infants and music. She is often depicted as a woman with a cow's head, wearing the headdress of two plumes and a solar disc decorated with stars symbolizing her role as a sky-goddess.

HAUS-SCHMIEDLEIN
See WICHTLEIN.

HECATE
Greek moon-goddess, Neo-Pagan goddess of fertility and moon-magick, Queen of the Underworld, and protectress of all Witches. Hecate is the Crone aspect of the Triple Goddess. She is also known as both the "Goddess of Darkness and Death" and the "Queen of Ghosts and Crossroads," and is identified with the Greek goddess Persephone.

HELIOMANCY
The art and practice of divination by the sun.

HELL-BROTH
In medieval Witchcraft and sorcery, the nickname for a magickal potion boiled in a cauldron and consisting of various repulsive ingredients such as animal entrails, urine, powdered skulls, black widow spiders, etc.

HEMOMANCY
The ancient art and practice of divination by the blood of a sacrificed animal or person.

HENBANE
A poisonous, narcotic plant associated with sorcery and Witchcraft, and used as one of the main ingredients in the flying ointments of medieval Witches.

HEPATOSCOPY
The art and practice of divination by interpreting the liver of a sacrificed sheep. This form of divination was common among the Babylonians, Etruscans and Hittites.

HERMAPHRODITUS
In Greek mythology, the son of Hermes and Aphrodite, who, by becoming united in one body with a nymph,

possessed the sexual organs and physical characteristics of both man and woman.

HERMES
In Greek mythology, the god of commerce, invention, cunning and theft; identified with the Roman god Mercury. Hermes also served as messenger and herald for the other gods, as patron of travelers and rogues, and as the conductor of the dead to Hades. He was also the protector of the flocks, and was known for his speed, craftiness, and youthful nature.

HERMES TRISMEGISTUS
The Greek name for Thoth, the ancient Egyptian moon god and author of works on alchemy, astrology and magick. (Latin, from Greek *Hermes trismegistos*, meaning "Hermes the thrice greatest.")

HERMETIC
(1) Of or relating to Hermes Trismegistus. (2) Of or pertaining to the occult sciences, especially alchemy and Ceremonial Magick. (3) A magician or priest of the Hermetic tradition.

HERMETIC MAGICK
A form of magick, dating back to the first century A.D., that combines Egyptian magickal knowledge with other occult traditions.

HEX
(1) In American folk belief, an evil spell or curse. Hexing involves the casting of spells (usually by a professional sorcerer known as a "hex doctor") through magickal formulas based mainly on Gypsy folk magick and medieval church rituals. Although hexes are usually performed as black magick to inflict illness, misfortune or

even death, they can also be used in a positive manner to cure sickness, bring good luck, or break the powers of the evil eye and the jinx. The belief in hexerai (the Pennsylvania Dutch version of sorcery) continues to be widespread in modern times. As late as 1949, a lawsuit for "alienation of affections by hexing" was brought in Lehigh County, Pennsylvania. Hex signs, which are painted on barns to protect animals from the evil eye and the workings of spells, are still common today in eastern Pennsylvania. The term "hex" is found in various parts of the United States, especially among the Pennsylvania Dutch, and stems from the German *hexe*, meaning witch. (2) To bewitch or cast an evil spell upon a particular person, animal or property. (3) A man or woman who practices evil folk magick or possesses the supernatural power of the evil eye.

HEXAGRAM
In Western magick and mysticism, a powerful occult symbol made up of two triangles, one superimposed on the other, and used to master spirits and banish influences of evil. The two triangles symbolize man and God; the symbol of the "Seal of Solomon" or the "Star of David"; in alchemy, the triangles symbolize the elements of Fire and Water, distillation, and the Philosopher's Stone which is said to be composed of both fire and water.

HEX SIGN
In Pennsylvania Dutch folk belief, a brightly-colored symbol of a five, six, or eight-pointed star within a circle, described as a "painted prayer." Hex signs, at one time known as *sechs*, are painted on the sides of barns and on the doors and window shutters of farmhouses in many parts of eastern Pennsylvania to protect

the home, farm or animals against sorcery and to keep evil spirits at bay.

HEXTER
A hex-doctor; a person who makes magickal antidotes such as amulets and talismans to ward off the evil power of hexes.

HIEROMANCY
The art and practice of divination by drawing prophetic conclusions from objects of ancient sacrifice. It is also called Haruspicy.

HIGH MAGICK
Ceremonial Magick.

HIPPOMANCY
The art and practice of divination by horses. It was practiced among the Celts who symbolically interpreted the gaits of white horses.

HOLEY STONES
In folk-magic, small stones with naturally occurring holes that are strung together on a thick cord like a necklace and hung in a window as an amulet to attract good luck and keep evil influences away from a house.

HOODOO
A type of folk magick which combines European techniques with the Voodoo rituals brought to the New World by African slaves. Hoodoo is practiced mainly by African Americans in rural areas of the southern United States, especially Louisiana.

HOODOO HANDS
In hoodoo, magickal charms used to bring the wearer good luck, or to bring illness and death if directed against an enemy.

HORARY ASTROLOGY
An astrological method that uses charts for answering questions and/or solving specific problems. See also ASTROLOGY.

HORNED GOD
In Witchcraft and Wicca, the consort of the Goddess and the symbol of male sexuality. The Horned God of the Witches is usually identified with the Greek nature-god Pan or Cernunnos, the Celtic lord of wild animals.

HOROSCOPE
In astrology, a chart of the heavenly bodies that shows the relative positions of the planets at a certain moment in time. Given the exact time and place of an individual's birth, an astrologer can cast a horoscope from which he or she can define the subject's character and advise them on future courses of action.

HOROSCOPY
The art and practice of divination by casting astrological horoscopes.

HORUS
Ancient Egyptian god of the sky, and son of Isis and Osiris. He is depicted as a falcon-headed man with the sun and moon as his eyes.

HOUNFOR
In Voodoo, a clearing on which peristyle sanctuaries for loas have been erected.

HOUNGAN
In Voodoo, a priest who summons loas and works magick. The term derives from the Fon language of Dahomey and Togo and means literally "the master of a god."

HOUNSIS
In Voodoo, an initiate.

HUAKANKI
Phallus-shaped pieces of alabaster used by magicians in Bolivia as powerful love-attracting amulets.

HYDROMANCY
The art and practice of divination by water and by things dropped into water. The following methods are just a few examples of hydromancy: predicting future events by interpretation of the rings formed on the surface of a cup of water into which a gemstone, ring or amulet has been dropped; gazing into a pail of water to locate lost or stolen objects or to see the face of a thief; drawing omens by observing all details of the water in a stream or river, such as the direction of its flow, its movement, and whether it is calm or restless. Hydromancy has been practiced since ancient times in nearly every area of the world, but most commonly in New Guinea, Scandinavia, Takiti and the Hawaiian islands.

HYDROMANTIA
A hydromantic form of divination in which a seer or inquirer gazes fixedly into a cup or pool of still water to see the future or to make gods, demons or spirits appear in the water. Other forms of hydromantic divination include lecanomancy (divination by basins of water), oinomancy (divination by lees of wine), and pegomancy (divination by bubbling fountains of water).

I CHING (THE BOOK OF CHANGES):

An ancient Chinese science of synchronicity, dating back to the very beginning of Chinese civilization, which is based on a group of 64 6-line drawings called hexagrams that describe the patterns of change and transformation. I Ching (pronounced ee-jing) teaches that the womb of the universe is a limited imperceptible void—T'ai Chi, the Absolute. In it everything has its being, and each owes its individuality to a particular combination of Yin (negative) and Yang (positive). To consult the I Ching for advice or answers to questions, three coins are tossed or a counting game with fifty yarrow sticks is played in order to randomly produce one of the hexagrams. When properly interpreted, the hexagrams reveal either fortune or misfortune which can be used in divination and for personal consultation.

ICHTHYOMANCY

The art and practice of divination by interpreting the entrails of a fish.

IDOL

An image or inanimate object representing a god or goddess. In certain beliefs, an idol is thought to possess power in itself and is often worshipped in rituals as if it was the actual deity.

IDOLATER

One who worships idols.

IDUN

In Teutonic mythology, the goddess of spring who possessed the golden apples of eternal youth. She was the consort of Bragi, the god of poetry, and lived in Asgard, the sacred space reserved for the abode of the gods and goddesses. (She was also known as Idhunn, Ithunn, and Ithun.)

ILLUMINATION
Mystical or spiritual enlightenment.

ILMARINEN
Finnish god of wind and good weather.

IMAGE MAGICK
A primitive but potent form of magick, which works on the basic principle that like produces like. The most common objects used in this practice are small enchanted figures created to represent enemies in the belief that anything done to the effigy similarly affects the man or woman whom it represents. These figures, or image dolls, can be made of wax or clay, carved of wood, or plaited from straw. Wax image dolls are most commonly used since they can easily kill an enemy by being placed in a fire or over a candle to melt, dissolved in hot water to cause the victim a prolonged, agonizing death, or stuck with pins, nails or blades to make various parts of the victim's body burn with excruciating pain. A sorcerer can also use an image doll to bring impotency, blindness or insanity to an enemy simply by stabbing the appropriate body part of the doll. The practice of image magick is common among practitioners of Voodoo and African tribal magick. Although image dolls are generally associated with black magick and evil sorcery, they can also be used in love magick and in white (or positive) magick rituals to heal sickness, stimulate fertility, etc. (Also called SYMPATHETIC MAGICK)

IMBOLC
One of the four Grand Witches' Sabbats. See CANDLE-MAS.

IMILOZI
In Zulu religion and folklore, ancestral spirits who communicate with the living by whistling.

IMMORTAL
A deity.

IMMORTALITY
Eternal life.

IMP
In medieval Witchcraft, a Witch's familiar; a small demon or goblin-like creature.

IMPRECATION
A curse; the act of invoking a curse upon.

INANNA
Sumerian goddess of love and war, identified with the Babylonian goddess Ishtar.

INARI
Japanese god of rice and harvest.

INCANTATION
The ritual recitation of words of power or special phrases, usually rhymed, in order to produce a magickal effect.

INCANTATRIX
A Witch or sorceress.

INCUBUS
In medieval folk-legend, a demon or evil spirit that takes on the shape of a handsome man and seduces women as they sleep in order to possess their souls. The female equivalent of the incubus is the succubus.

INTI RAIMI
The winter solstice feast celebrated by the Incas.

INVOCATION
In Ceremonial Magick, the act of summoning or conjuring a spirit, angel, demon or deity by means of sacred god-names and/or words of power

ISHTAR
Assyrian, Babylonian and Neo-Pagan goddess of love, fertility and war who personifies the planet Venus. She is a Mother-Goddess and the consort of Tammuz. The crescent moon is one of her sacred symbols and she is depicted as a woman with bird-like facial features and braided hair, wearing bull's horns and jeweled necklaces, bracelets and anklets. She is identified with the Sumerian goddess Inanna and the Phoenician goddess Astarte.

ISIS
Ancient Egyptian goddess of fertility and Neo-Pagan goddess of magick and enchantment. In Egyptian mythology, Isis was the sister and consort of the sun-god Osiris, and was at times identified with the goddess Hathor. She is the symbol of divine motherhood and was regarded in her mysteries as the single form of all gods and goddesses. Isis is often called the "Goddess of Ten Thousand Names" and in Hellespont (now Dardanelles) she was known as Mystis, the Lady of the Mysteries.

ITHYPHALLIC
(1) A term used to describe sculptural representations and other religious images possessing exaggerated sexual organs, and associated with the worship of the phallus as an embodiment of generative power. (2) of or pertaining to the phallus carried in the ancient Roman orgy-festival of Bacchus known as the Bacchanalia. (3) relating to the sacred hymns to the wine-god Bacchus.

JAINA CROSS
A sacred and magickal symbol of the Jains resembling a swastika

JALJOGINI
In Punjab Indian folklore, an evil spirit which haunts streams and wells, and uses black magick to bring diseases to women and children

JANUS
Roman god of gates and doorways, and a deity associated with journeys and the beginning of things. He is depicted as having two faces, each looking in opposite directions.

JINGO
The summoning call of a conjurer.

JINNI
According to Moslem legend, a spirit-like creature of a higher order than humans who grants wishes. He is capable not only of assuming human form but also of exercising supernatural influences over human beings. (Also, djinn, djinni, djinny, genie, jinn.)

JINX
A person or thing that is believed to attract bad luck or misfortune; to bring bad luck or misfortune to.

JETTATURA
An Italian term used to describe a person possessed by the power of the evil eye.

JOSS
A Chinese idol.

JOSS HOUSE
In traditional Chinese religious practice, a sacred temple or shrine containing idols.

JOSS STICK
In traditional Chinese religious practice, a special stick of fragrant incense burnt in ritual offerings to appease the gods and to drive away evil spirits and negative influences.

JUJU
In West African magick, an object used as an amulet; magickal charm or fetish by sorcerers; African magickal rites involving witch doctors, black magick and the casting out of demons from possessed persons and places.

JUMBY
A term used by Caribbeans for the ghost of a dead person.

JUPITER
Roman god of wisdom, thunder and lightning, identified with the Greek god Zeus; in astrology, the planetary ruler of the zodiac signs Sagittarius and Pisces.

JURUA
In Andaman Island folklore, an evil sea spirit which is believed to attack fishermen with invisible illness-causing spears. (Also known as Juruwin.)

JUTURNA
In Roman mythology, a nymph of healing springs and wells, and a protectress against fire. A sacred feast, the Juturnalia, was celebrated in her honor on the eleventh day of January in Rome.

KABBALAH
A secret occult theosophy of rabbinical origin based on esoteric interpretations of the Hebrew Scriptures. It appears as an elaborate system of magick, but is actually a tool for achieving mystic union with God. The Kabbalah teaches that there are 72 different names of God and that the universe is made up of four planes of being. (Also spelled Cabala, Cabbala, Kabala and Qabbalah.)

KABBALIST
One who practices the Kabbalah.

KACHES
In Armenian folk belief, a group of violent spirits who live in stony places, steal wine and grain, and torture humans.

KAKAMORA
In Melanesian folklore, a race of man-eating supernatural beings that lives in caves, holes and banyan trees.

KALI
In Hinduism, the goddess of death, consort of Shiva, and the personification of the dark and terrifying forces of nature. She is depicted in art as a fanged, dark-skinned warrior woman wearing a necklace of human skulls around her neck. She is also known as the Black One, Chandi, Durga, Parvati, Sati, and Uma.

KAMA
In Hinduism, the god of love and desire.

KAPPA
In Japanese folk belief, a malicious, man-eating spirit with the head of a monkey, the body of a tortoise, and the arms and legs of a frog.

KARMA
The law of cause-and-effect that applies to all of our actions and their consequences in this life or in future incarnations.

KARTTIKEYA
In Hindu mythology, the six-faced god of war, and ruler of the planet Mars.

KAUKAS
In Lithuanian folklore, a dwarf-like household spirit.

KELPIES
In Scottish folklore, mischievous water-spirits that take the form of a black or gray horse and are said to lead astray or devour travelers who mount them to cross a river or stream.

KEPHALONOMANCY
The art and practice of divination among the Lombards in which lighted carbon was poured on the baked head of an ass or goat as the names of suspected criminals were called out. If a crackling occurred, it was believed that the man or woman whose name had been called out was guilty as charged.

KERES
In Greek mythology, omnipresent spiritual beings who were believed to have escaped from Pandora's box. The Keres brought diseases and ills to mankind, served the gods, and dragged off the corpses of the dead.

KEY OF SOLOMON
Title of a famous medieval grimoire containing conjurations, prayers, detailed pentacles for each of the planets, and detailed commentaries on the nature of spirits

invoked in ceremonial magick, Witchcraft and necromancy.

KHONS
One of the sacred moon-gods of ancient Egypt. He was also worshipped as a god of healing.

KI
Sumerian earth mother.

KOBOLDS
In German folklore, malignant gnome-like creatures who haunted old houses and underground mines. In certain regions of Germany, the kobolds were said to be cheerful domestics devoted to mortal hearths and homes. However, they were known to cause utter chaos if ignored or abused by their chosen human family.

KORNBOCK
In German folklore, elusive fairy-like spirits who guard grain and also cause it to ripen. The Kornbock were said to ride the breezes that rippled the wheat fields, hide among the stalks in the guise of blue cornflowers, and prowl the fields in the form of ill-tempered goats.

KNOCKERS
See WICHTLEIN.

KNUCKER
In English country folklore, a type of swamp dragon which inhabits marshes and foul, bottomless pits nicknamed "knucker holes."

KNUCKER HOLE
In English country folklore, a watery, bottomless pit where ferocious swamp dragons known as knuckers

were believed to dwell. The knucker holes, which gave off an eerie mist, were said to always be ice-cold in the summer and steaming hot in the winter.

KRONOS
Greek god of time and ruler of the universe, identified with the Roman god Saturn. (Also spelled Cronus.)

KRU
A Cambodian shaman who uses various herbs and gemstones to exorcise evil spirits which are believed to bring disease to mankind.

KUAN TI
Chinese war god whose festival is celebrated on May 13th.

KUAN YIN
Chinese goddess of fertility, childbirth and compassion.

KUBERA
In Hindu folklore and mythology, the god of wealth and lord of the treasures of the earth. He is depicted as a deformed three-legged man with eight teeth.

KUKULCAN
Mayan storm god depicted as a green feathered serpent with the teeth of a jaguar. His sacred feast, the Chick-aban, was celebrated in the month of October.

KUNDALINI YOGA
A branch of Yoga that teaches integration through the physical and mental control of a dormant energy in the human body referred to as the Kundalini.

KUPALA
Slavic goddess of life, sex and vitality who is wor-shipped on Midsummer's Day.

LABRYS
In Goddess-worship, a double-headed axe used to symbolize the Goddess in Her lunar aspect.

LAICA
Among the Aymara Indians of Bolivia, a magician or practitioner of sorcery.

LAKA
Hawaiian rainstorm goddess and patroness of hula dancers.

LAKSHMI
In Hindu mythology, the goddess of the lotus and consort of the god Vishnu.

LAMIA
(1) In Greek mythology, a horrible monster represented as a serpent with the head and breasts of a woman, and reputed to prey upon humans, suck the blood of babies, and feed on the flesh of corpses. (2) in medieval folk-legend, a vampiric fairy-creature who appears in numerous threatening guises. Although the lamia represented the darkest side of Faerie, they often took on the form of beautiful women or mermaids whose natures were amorous and haunted by a yearning love for mortal men. (3) a sorceress or female vampire.

LAMMAS
One of the four Grand Witches' Sabbats. Also known as Lughnasadh and August Eve, it is the first festival of Harvest and is celebrated on August 1st. Lammas was originally celebrated by the ancient Druids as Lughnasadh to pay homage to Lugh, the Celtic sun god. In other pre-Christian cultures, it was commemorated as a festival of bread and as a day to honor the

death of the Sacred King. On Lammas, homemade breads and berry pies are traditionally baked and eaten in honor of the harvest. The making of corn dollies is another old custom associated with the Lammas Sabbat. See also CORN DOLLY.

LAMPADOMANCY
The art and practice of divination based on the observation of the movements of a lamp's flame.

LEANAN-SIDE
In Irish folklore, a nocturnal "fairy mistress" who drains the life and breath from her human lovers like a succubus.

LECANOMANCY
The art and practice of divination by casting objects into basins of water and then interpreting the resulting images and sounds; a form of hydromancy.

LEFT-HAND PATH
The practice of black magick and sorcery.

LEGBA
In Voodoo, the Rada loa of pathways and crossroads. (In the Voudoun religion, any and all crosses possess symbolic meaning.) Originally a Dahomean sun god, Legba is the most important loa, for every Rada ceremony must begin with an invocation to him. He is not only the interpreter of the other loas, allowing them to rise up through a ceremonial stake plunged into the ground, but also the guardian and keeper of the keys that unlock the gate separating the material world of man from the world of spirit. Legba is envisaged as a limping, poorly-dressed old peasant man who smokes a pipe and walks on a crutch. He is enormously powerful,

and it is said that possession of an entranced devotee by him is extraordinarily violent, causing the person's limbs to be contorted as if crippled and the face to become ancient-looking and weary. In his Petro form, Legba is called Carrefour, the master of the crossroads. Tuesday is his sacred day.

LEMURES
In spiritualism, spirits of the dead that manifest during seances causing rappings and other phenomena; elemental spirits of Air.

LEO
In astrology, the fifth sign of the zodiac, symbolized by the lion. Leo is a fire sign, and is ruled by the Sun. Arrogance, flamboyance, generosity, pride and vitality are typical Leo traits.

LEPANTHROPY
The ability to change from human to rabbit or hare by means of charms, magickal incantations or supernatural powers. See also ZOOMORPHISM.

LEPRECHAUN
In Irish country folklore, a roguish, elfin creature who cobbles, haunts wine cellars, and hoards treasure. He appears as a bearded, dwarf-like man wearing a tall hat with a gold buckle, and smoking a pipe. It was said that a leprechaun had to reveal the location of his hidden pot of gold if caught by a human, and although the creature was sometimes captured, no mortal ever succeeded in stealing his fabled treasure: The clever leprechaun would trick his captors into looking the other way, and then vanish in a wink.

LESHY (also LESHIYE)
In Russian folklore, shape-shifting forest fairies who are mischievous and sometimes hostile to mortals

LEVITATION
The raising and floating of objects or people by means of supernatural forces, magick or telekinetic powers

LIBANOMANCY
The art and practice of divination by the burning of frankincense. (Also spelled Livanomancy.)

LIBATION
In Witchcraft, Wicca and other Pagan religions, water or wine which is ritually poured on an altar, on the ground, or on a sacred fire as an offering to the Goddess, Horned God or other deity.

LIBRA
In astrology, the seventh sign of the zodiac, also known as the sign of the Scales or the Balance. Libra is an air sign, and is ruled by the planet Venus. Gentleness, honesty, fairness, indecision, and vanity are typical Libran traits.

LINDWORM
In folk-legend and mythology, a flightless dragon with a serpentine body and a pair of clawed legs.

LITHOBOLIA
Poltergeist-like spirits who bombard persons and/or dwellings with showers of stones or rocks.

LITHOMANCY
The art and practice of divination utilizing the reflections of color from precious stones or beads to draw

omens. A blue reflection signifies good luck; a black or gray one foretells misfortune; red indicates love and/or marriage; yellow means betrayal; purple signifies sorrow; green is the sign of success

LOA

In Voodoo, a spirit or deity that takes possession of a devotee in a state of trance. The two main types of loas are the Rada and the Petro. The Rada are protective loas of Dahomean and Nigerian derivation invoked in rituals of white magick. The Petros are aggressive loas named after the Spanish houngan Don Pedro and invoked mainly in rituals of black magick. There are also minor classes of loas and these include the Congo, the Nago, and the Wangol.

LOCO

In Voodoo, the loa of healing. Loco is also known as Papa Loko Dahomey and is the spirit of herbs and vegetation who gives healing power to leaves.

LOKI

Scandinavian god of fire.

LOUP GAROU

In Voodoo folk-legend, a werewolf or a person who possesses the supernatural ability to change into a wolf-like creature. See also LYCNATHROPY; WEREWOLF; ZOOMORPHISM.

LOVE POTION

In Witchcraft, an herbal aphrodisiac used in magickal spells with incantations to arouse love or sexual passion; a philtre.

LUCIFERANS
A medieval Satanic sect prevalent in the thirteenth century. The Luciferans worshipped the fallen angel Lucifer and were said to have sacrificed children and animals to demons in nocturnal rites.

LUCINA
Lunar goddess of ancient Rome associated with childbirth.

LUCK BALL
A hoodoo charm containing various ingredients wound in yarn, and worn to bring good luck.

LUGH
Early Celtic sun-god worshipped by the ancient Druids as the Bountiful Giver of Harvest. The Pagan sabbat festival of Lughnasadh (meaning "Commemoration of Lugh") was originated by the Druids to pay homage to the sun-god.

LUNA
Roman and Neo-Pagan moon-goddess whose name is Latin for "moon."

LUNATION
In astrology, the exact moment of the moon's conjunction with the sun; the time of the new moon.

LYCANTHROPE
A werewolf. See also LOUP GAROU; LYCANTHROPY; WEREWOLF; ZOOMORPHISM.

LYCANTHROPY
The supernatural or magickal ability to assume the physical form and characteristics of a wolf. The word stems from the Greek LUKOS, meaning "a wolf" and ANTHROPOS, meaning "a man."

MABON
The Autumn Equinox Sabbat.

MACHAROMANCY
The art and practice of divination by knives or swords.

MACHI
Among the Araucanian Indians, female shamans who cure the sick by means of suction and massage. Although in modern times the machi shamans are women, in the past the machi were men who dressed in women's costumes when healing ill or bewitched patients.

MACUMBA
A Voodoo-like religion practiced in Brazil and consisting of Haitian folk-beliefs, African animism, Latin American spiritualism and aspects of Christianity.

MAGE
A Master Magician. (See CEREMONIAL MAGICK.)

MAGICIAN
A non-religious practitioner of ceremonial or ritual magick; one who summons elementals, demons or spirits to work magick but does not worship deities, celebrate Sabbats or follow any Wiccan tradition.

MAGICK
The art, science and practice of producing "supernatural" effects, causing change to occur in conformity, and controlling events in Nature with will. As a tool of Witchcraft, the old spelling of the word with a final "K" is used to distinguish it from the magic of stage conjuring and illusion which has nothing to do with ceremonial workings or the magickal states of consciousness produced by ritual.

MAGICK CANDLE
In medieval sorcery, a special candle composed of hu
man tallow, and used by sorcerers and diviners as a
divinatory tool to locate buried treasure. It was believed
that when the candle sparkled brightly with a good deal
of noise, it was a sign that treasure was close by. The
closer one approached the treasure, the brighter the
candle would sparkle, going out completely when directly above the spot where the treasure was buried.

MAGICK SQUARES
In Abramelin magick, powerful magickal talismans
made from rows of numbers or letters of the alphabet
arranged so that the words may read horizontally or
vertically as palindromes and the numbers total the
same when added up in either direction. In order for a
magick square to work properly, it must include every
consecutive number from one until the square is filled,
and according to the rules of numerology, each number
can only be used once.

MAHUIKA
Polynesian underworld goddess of earthquakes and
fire.

MAISO
In Paressi Indian mythology, the woman of stone who
created the world.

MAKARA
In Hindu mythology and folklore, a crab-like sea monster. In the Hindu zodiac, the makara represents the
astrological sign of Capricorn.

MALEDICT
In sorcery and black magick, to pronounce a curse against; to hex or direct negative psychic energy against another person with evil intent.

MALEDICTION
A curse or hex.

MALEFICIA
(1) Misfortunes, injuries, sicknesses or calamities that are attributed to the vindictive malice of evil sorcerers. (2) black magick or evil bewitchment.

MALEFICS
In astrology, planets whose influences are said to be negative such as Mars and Saturn.

MALKIN
A Witch's familiar in the form of a cat. (See also FAMILIAR.)

MAMA-COCHA
Peruvian sea goddess and patroness of fishermen.

MAMBO
A Voodoo priestess who directs the worship of loas at ceremonies. She also possesses the power to heal sick or injured people using white magick, divine the future and create zombies with black magick.

MANCY
A suffix derived from the Greek MANTEIA, meaning "divination."

MANDRAGORA
(1) In herbalism, a mandrake plant or root. (2) In folklore, spirits or demons in the form of tiny, beardless

men with black skin who roam among humans and assist sorcerers in the practice of black magic.

MANDRAKE
A poisonous, narcotic plant associated with medieval Witchcraft and sorcery, and believed to be the most magickal of all plants and herbs. It is potent in all forms of enchantment and is regarded as a powerful aphrodisiac by the Orientals. Mandrake, ruled by the planet Venus, possesses purple flowers and a narcotic-producing human-shaped root which, according to legend, screams when it is plucked from the soil. There are "male" mandrakes with roots shaped like a man's body, and "female" mandrakes with roots that resemble the body of a woman. In ancient times, Europeans and Asians alike believed that powerful familiar-spirits inhabited the plant—a belief arising out of the likeness of its root to the human form. Mandrake has been used in spells and rituals to increase psychic powers as well as in love spells, fertility rites and sorcery. The roots have also been used to divine the future. It is said that they shake their heads when questions are put to them. Caution should always be exercised when using mandrake in potions, brews and philtres for it is a very magickal plant and misuse of it can result in sickness, delirium or slow, agonizing death.

MANEKI NEKO
A cat-shaped good-luck charm used by Japanese shopkeepers to attract customers.

MANES
In Roman mythology, spirits of the dead who inhabit the Underworld and are ruled by Mania, the goddess of the dead.

MANI
In Indian folklore, a valuable magick jewel (transparent beryl) believed to be found in the head of a cobra, and used as a powerful amulet against all evil and negative forces.

MANISM
The worship of the spirits of the dead.

MANITOU
A nature-spirit with great magickal power for either good or evil, deified in the religion of the Algonquin Indians of North America.

MANTIC
Of, pertaining to, or possessing the power of divination; prophetic.

MANTICORE (also MANTICHORA)
A man-eating supernatural creature which, according to folk-legend of India, had a human head, the body of a lion, and the tail of a scorpion or dragon. The manticore possessed great strength, triple rows of sharp fangs, and a tail containing a cluster of deadly poisoned barbs.

MANTRA
In Hinduism, a sacred chant or sound intoned silently as part of a meditation ritual, often to achieve union with the Divine.

MANTRA YOGA
A branch of yoga that uses the chanting of sacred words or sounds to achieve union with the Godhead.

MARA
In folklore, a female elf.

MARGARITOMANCY
The art and practice of divination by pearls. The word stems from the Greek MARGARITES, meaning "pearls." This form of divination was a common practice in Africa, Polynesia and the Hawaiian islands.

MARRE
In Haitian Voodoo, a term used to denote proper control of a loa by a devotee.

MARS
(1) The Roman god of war. (2) In astrology, the planetary ruler of the signs Aries and Scorpio.

MASAN
In Hindu folk belief, a grotesque black demon or ghost (often the spirit of a dead child) who inhabits the ashes of a funeral pyre.

MASAUWU
The Hopi Indian god of death, war, fire and night.

MAY DAY
See BELTANE.

MAY EVE
See BELTANE.

MEDICINE BAG
See MOJO BAG.

MEDICINE DANCE
Among the Plains Indians of North America, a ritual dance performed in order to obtain supernatural assistance.

MEDICINE LODGE
Among many North American Indian tribes, a large wooden structure used for various ritualistic ceremonies.

MEDICINE MAN
In primitive societies, a shaman or witch-doctor believed to possess supernatural powers for healing, invoking spirit guides, preparing effective magickal remedies, and exorcising evil spirits from possessed persons.

MEDITATION
In various religions, including Wicca, a technique of mind control that produces a feeling of tranquility and peacefulness, and often leads to transcendental awareness.

MEDIUM
In spiritualism, a gifted person through whom the spirits of the dead speak and act during a seance.

MELUSINE
In folk-legend and heraldry, a two-tailed mermaid or water-spirit.

MENTAL TELEPATHY
See TELEPATHY.

MERCURY
(1) In Roman mythology, the messenger of the gods, identified with the Greek god Hermes. (2) In astrology, the planetary ruler of the signs Gemini and Virgo. (3) In alchemy, a term for quicksilver.

MERKHET
A dowsing pyramid consisting of an ellipsoidal rock suspended from an L-shaped wooden beam and used by priests of ancient Egypt as a device to focus energy and as a tool for astrological calculations and land surveying to help establish the locations for sacred temples of magick and worship.

MERMAID
A fabled, bewitching creature of the sea having the upper body of a beautiful naked woman and the tail of a fish.

MERMAN
A male mermaid having the upper body of a bearded man and the scaly tail of a fish.

MESMERISM
Hypnotism.

METAGNOMY
A modern form of intuitive divination of the past, present and future while under a hypnotic trance.

METEMPSYCHOSIS
The transmigration or reincarnation of human souls into animal bodies after death and vice versa.

METEOROMANCY
The art and practice of drawing omens from meteors and similar phenomena.

METOPOSCOPY
The art and practice of analyzing a person's character or predicting future events by reading the lines of the forehead.

MEZUZAH

In Judaism, a small piece of parchment inscribed with certain Biblical passages and rolled up in a container affixed to a door frame as a magickal charm to protect the house and family against demons and evil ghosts. The mezuzah can also be worn or carried as a protective amulet The use of door-charms date back to ancient Egypt where small tablets engraved with hieroglyphic spells ("pillars of Horus") were placed on doors to frighten away malignant spirits of the dead.

MIDSUMMER

See SUMMER SOLSTICE SABBAT.

MIN

Ancient Egyptian god of fertility and protector of travelers.

MIND BENDER

A hypnotist.

MIND-BENDING

Hypnotism; mesmerism.

MIND-READING

See TELEPATHY.

MINOTAUR

(1) A monster with the body of a man and the head of a bull. (2) in Greek mythology, the son of Pasiphae by a sacred bull, slain by Theseus.

MISTLETOE

A parasitic plant associated with the oak tree and considered sacred to the god Apollo. At one time it was believed to possess special virtues as a healer and was given the nickname of all-heal. The ancient Druids regarded the mistletoe as a very powerful plant and used it in their solemn fertility rites. Clad in white robes, they used a golden sickle to cut and gather it on the sixth day of the new moon. Mistletoe has long been associated with the Winter Solstice and is symbolic of the sun's rebirth. Its power for good is said to be the greatest when it is gathered on Saint John's Eve. In medieval England, mistletoe was hung in stables to protect horses against evil and sorcery, while in Sweden, the withered, yellow branches of the plant were used as divining rods by dowsers to locate buried treasure. According to dream interpreters, when mistletoe appears in a dream, it is an omen of good health, happiness and great rejoicing.

MITHRA
In Persian mythology, the powerful and widely worshipped god of light, truth and justice, whose six-day feast, the Mihrajan, was held annually in the month of September.

MOJO BAG
A small leather or flannel bag filled with a variety of magickal items such as herbs, stones, feathers, bones, etc., and carried or worn as a charm to attract or dispel certain influences.

MOON
In Witchcraft and Wicca, the sacred symbol of the Goddess and also a symbol of magick, fertility and the secret powers of Nature. In astrology, the planetary rule of the sign Cancer.

MOONCHILD
In astrology, a person born under the sign of Cancer.

MORPHEUS
In Greek mythology, the god of dreams, now existing in popular literary allusion as the god of sleep.

MORRIGAN
Celtic war-goddess of death and destruction. According to mythology, she appears in the form of a raven (a bird of ill-omen in the Celtic tradition) before and during battles. As a Goddess Trinity, she was known as Macha when she worked magick with the blood of the slain; Badb when she appeared in the form of a giantess on the eve of war to warn soldiers of their fates; and Neman when she appeared as a shape-shifting crone.

MOSS MAIDENS
In German folklore, beneficent fairies with old, furrowed faces who weave moss to dress the roots of trees, and are wise in the healing properties of plants.

MOTHER GODDESS
In various pantheons, a deity worshipped as a goddess of fertility, birth, or sexual union.

MRIGANKA
In Indian folk belief, a bright and shining magickal sword which endows its possessor with the power to conquer and control the world.

MUGWORT
An herb associated with Witchcraft and healing. It is known as "Saint John's plant" in Holland and Germany as its powers are said to be the most potent when it is gathered on Saint John's Eve. According to legend, a girdle made of mugwort was worn by John the Baptist to protect him from harm in the wilderness. A sachet filled with mugwort is said to offer a traveler protection

against fatigue, sunstroke, wild beasts and evil spirits. A pillow stuffed with mugwort induces psychic dreams. In China during the time of the Dragon Festival (the fifth day of the fifth moon), mugwort is hung up to keep away evil demons, while in other parts of the world, a special crown made from the sprays of the plant protects the wearer against possession by demonic forces. Brewed as a tea, often with lemon balm, mugwort is consumed to aid divination, meditation and psychic development. Mugwort tea is also used by many Witches as a ceremonial potion for Samhain and full moon rituals, and as a wash to cleanse and consecrate crystal balls, magick mirrors and quartz crystal amulets and wands.

MUMBO JUMBO
(1) Among the Mandingo peoples of the western Sudan in Africa, a priest or shaman who possesses the supernatural power to protect his village from sorcery and evil spirits. The word Mumbo Jumbo derives from the Mandingo *ma-ma-gyo-mbo*, meaning "magician who makes the troubled spirits of ancestors go away." (2) An object possessing supernatural or magickal powers; a fetish. (3) Any meaningless or pretentious magickal ritual; an unintelligible incantation.

MUT
Ancient Egyptian goddess of fertility.

MYLITTA
An ancient Babylonian fertility goddess, identified with Ishtar and Aphrodite, to whom women sacrificed their virginity. Her name means "she who causes to bear."

MYOMANCY
The art and practice of divination by interpreting the cries or particular activities of rats or mice. This form of

divination was a common practice in ancient Egypt, Rome and Assyria.

MYSTIC
One who practices spiritual discipline aiming at union with the Godhead or Supreme Being through meditation, trancelike contemplation or self-surrender.

NAGALISM
The ancient occult practice of serpent-worship.

NAIAD
In Greek mythology, a type of nymph living in and presiding over rivers, springs and fountains; a water-nymph.

NAIRYOSANGHA
Iranian god of fire.

NAKK
In Estonian folklore, an evil water spirit who appears in the guise of a human or an animal, and devours its victims after bewitching them with its singing.

NANIGA
A Voodoo-like religious cult in Cuba that uses hypnotic chanting and dancing to invoke African deities.

NATAL CHART
In astrology, a special map showing the positions of the sun, moon and planets at the exact moment of an individual's birth.

NAVKY
In Slavic folklore, the spirits of unbaptized or murdered children who appear as baby girls rocking in tree branches and wailing in the night. It is said that some navky beg passersby for baptism, while other, more vengeful ones lure unwitted travelers into dangerous places. In Yugoslavia, the navky are said to appear in the form of great black birds whose cries could chill the soul of a man.

NECROMANCY
The ancient occult method of forecasting the future through communication with spirits of the dead; the art and practice of divination by spirits.

NEMESIS
Greek goddess of anger and vengeance. In mythology, the daughter of Erebus and Nyx.

NEPHELOMANCY
The art and practice of divination by interpreting the shape and direction of clouds.

NEPTUNE
Roman god of the sea, brother of Zeus, and equivalent of the Greek sea-god Poseidon. In astrology, one of the planetary rulers of the zodiac sign Pisces.

NHANG
In Armenian folklore, a demonic river-spirit which appears in the guise of a woman and sucks the blood of its human victims, usually swimmers.

NIGROMANCY
Black magick; necromancy.

NIKE
Greek goddess of victory.

NIMBUS
In Classical Iconography, a cloudy luminescence surrounding a deity when on earth; the aura of a god or goddess.

NINGWOT
A method of divination practiced in Burma that uses a heated bamboo stem to foretell future events or answer questions.

NINGYO
In Japanese folklore, a supernatural being resembling a mermaid.

NIRRIT
In Vedic mythology, an evil goddess associated with the Hindu Kali. She personifies destruction, and is believed to be the bringer of diseases.

NISSE
In Scandinavian folk belief, ancestral household spirits who can either be helpful or mischievous. (Compare with BROWNIE, DOMOVIK, and KOBOLDS.)

NIXIES
In Scandinavian folklore, hostile water-spirits that appear in the form of dwarves or centaurs and lure people to their death by drowning.

NJORD
Scandinavian god of the sea and prosperity. The patron of fishermen.

NOCNITSA
In Polish, Russian, Serbian and Slovak folklore, a hideous "night-hag" who torments small children with nightmares. She is also known as Krisky or Plasky.

NOIDE
A shaman of the Lapps who uses a magick drum to communicate with spirits of the dead.

NOVEMBER EVE
See SAMHAIN.

NUDIDA
In Dahomean Voodoo, a small sack containing red and white kola and powder, and soaked in the blood of a

pigeon. The nudida is used by mamboes and houngans as a magickal charm to cure colic.

NUMEROLOGY
An ancient and sacred method of divination that analyzes the symbolism of numbers and ascribes numerical values to the letters of the alphabet.

NUT
Ancient Egyptian sky-goddess and mother of Osiris, Isis, Set and Nephthys. (Also spelled Nuit.)

NYMPH
In Classical mythology and folk belief, a fairy-like nature spirit who usually appears in the form of a young, beautiful woman. There are three main classes of nymphs: the dryads (tree nymphs), the naiads (water nymphs), and the oreads (mountain nymphs).

NYMPHLET
A young nymph.

NYMPHOLEPSY
A frenzied state of mind or obsession induced by having seen or touched a nymph.

NYMPHOLEPT
A person in a state of nympholepsy.

NYX
Greek goddess of night and darkness. In mythology, the sister and consort of Erebus, the lord of darkness.

OBEAH
A form of sorcery, originating in Africa, that involves the use of fetishes. (Also spelled Obi.)

OBEAH-MAN
In Africa, a magician who practices black magick.

OBI
See OBEAH.

OBSESSION
In sorcery, the state of being beset or actuated by an evil spirit or demon without being physically possessed.

THE OCCULT
The spiritual sciences.

OCCULTA
A name given to the secret ceremonies of the esoteric mystery cults which, in medieval times, became almost synonymous with magickal practices, witchcraft, heresy, etc.

OCCULTATION
In astrology, the eclipsing of a planet by the moon or other celestial sphere.

OCCULTISM
The study of occult powers, supernatural influences, and other phenomena beyond the realm of ordinary human comprehension.

OCCULTIST
A person who studies or practices any form of divination, magick, mysticism, spiritualism or Theosophy.

OCEANIDES
Sea-nymphs.

OCULOMANCY
The art and practice of divination by interpretation of the size, shape or color of the eyes.

OD FORCE
See ODIC FORCE.

ODIC FORCE
An energy phenomenon which emanates from magnets and crystals, and is perceived by psychic sensitive persons as a blue (negative) or yellowish-red (positive) glowing light. It can be physically transferred from one substance to another and from one person to another. Odic Force, sometimes called *Od Force* or *Od* for short, was discovered by a German scientist named Baron Karl von Reichenbach (1788–1869) who named it after the Scandinavian god Odin.

ODIN
Scandinavian and Neo-Pagan god of wisdom, magick, art and poetry. He is also known as the Lord of the Dead, and is the consort of the goddess Frigga. According to Norse mythology, Odin battled giants, seduced mortals and woke the dead in his quest for occult wisdom and absolute power. He is depicted as an old one-eyed man, wearing a magickal ring and riding an eight-legged horse. Odin is the equivalent of the Pagan-Germanic god Woden.

OEONISTICY
Same as ORNITHOMANCY.

OFFERING
In Wicca, Witchcraft and magick, a presentation made to the Goddess, Horned God or other deity as an act of religious worship or sacrifice. See LIBATION.

OGHAM
Rune-casting; an ancient Celtic system of divination based on the casting and reading of line patterns or characters carved into or painted on small stones, beans, pieces of wood or bones.

OGRE
In medieval folk-legend, a hideous man-eating giant or monster.

OGRESS
In medieval folk-legend, a female ogre.

OGOUN
In Voodoo, a Haitian/Nigerian Rada loa of war and fire who protects his worshippers from bullets or wounds inflicted by weapons. He strengthens his devotees by slapping them and lifting them up into the air. Wednesday is his sacred day, the sword is his symbol and red is his favorite color.

OINOMANCY
The art and practice of drawing omens from the different symbolic patterns formed by spilt wine.

THE OLD ONES
The gods of the Old Religion; in Wicca, all aspects of the Goddess and Her consort, the Horned God.

THE OLD RELIGION
See WITCHCRAFT.

OMEN
Any phenomenon or thing that is interpreted as a sign of good luck or misfortune.

OMPHILOMANCY
The art and practice of divination by interpretation of the size and shape of the navel.

ONEIROMANCY
The art and practice of divination by interpretation of the symbolic or prophetic contents of dreams and nightmares.

ONOMATOMANCY
The art and practice of divination by interpreting the letters of a person's name. See NUMEROLOGY.

ONYCHOMANCY
The art and practice of divination by interpreting spots on the fingernails.

OOSCOPY
The art and practice of divination by eggs. To determine the gender of an unborn child, a pregnant woman would keep a chicken egg between her breasts until it hatched and then use the sex of the baby chick to determine the sex of her child. Divination by eggs is also known as Oomantia and Ovamancy.

OPHIOLATRY
The worship of serpents; negalism.

OPHIOMANCY
The art and practice of divination by serpents.

OPS
Ancient Roman goddess of fertility who was worshipped on August 25th at the Volcanalia and on December 19th at the Opalia.

ORACLE

A priest or person who transmits prophecies at a shrine consecrated to the worship and consultation of a prophetic deity.

OREADS

In Greek mythology, the class of nymphs who dwell in mountains, hills and grottoes.

ORGIA

A sacred winter ritual dedicated to the Greek god Dionysus, and consisting of wild, ecstatic dances and drunken festivity. The Orgia was the Greek version of the Roman orgy-festival, the Bacchanalia.

ORNITHOMANCY

The art and practice of divination by interpretation of the songs or flight patterns of birds. See AUGURY.

OSIRIS

Ancient Egyptian god of vegetation and fertility whose annual death and rebirth personified the self-renewing vitality and fertility of nature. He was also the Ruler of the Dead, and both the brother and consort of the goddess Isis. According to Egyptian mythology, Osiris was drowned and torn into fourteen pieces by his jealous brother Set, but then restored to life through the magickal powers of Isis.

OSTARA

One of the four Lesser Witches' Sabbats; the Spring Equinox Sabbat which occurs on or about March 21st. Ostara celebrates the birth of Spring and pays homage to Eostre, the Saxon fertility goddess.

OUIJA
In spiritualism, a method of spirit-communication consisting of a board with the letters of the alphabet, numbers and the words "yes" and "no" printed on it, and a
heart-shaped pointer called a planchette. After a specific question is asked, a spirit guides the hands of the
querant to move the planchette around the Ouija board,
spelling out words, names or spiritual messages.

OVOMANCY
The art and practice of divination by interpreting the
breakage of eggs placed over a fire.

OVERLOOK
To cast an evil spell or curse a victim by the power of the
evil eye. See also EVIL EYE and JETTATURA.

PAGAN
A word stemming from the Latin PAGANUS, meaning a "country dweller" and used derogatorily by the Church to describe a follower of the Old Religion, or any person who was not a Christian, Jew or Moslem; a follower of Wicca and other polytheistic religions.

PALMISTRY
See CHEIROMANCY.

PAN
Greek and Neo-Pagan horned-god of woodlands, fields, shepherds and fertility, often associated with the cult of Dionysus. Pan is depicted as a bearded man with the legs, horns and ears of a goat, and is the equivalent to the Roman nature deity Faunus.

P'AN CHIN LIEN
In Chinese mythology, the goddess of fornication, and patroness of prostitutes.

PAPA LEGBA
See LEGBA.

PARAPSYCHOLOGY
The branch of natural science that investigates extrasensory perception, psychokinesis and other psi phenomena not explainable by known scientific laws of nature.

PARAS
In Indonesian folk belief, a magickal stone which turns everything it touches into gold.

PARJANYA
The Vedic god of rain, lightning and thunder.

PARVATI
Hindu goddess of mountains, and the consort of Shiva. She is known as the ruler of elves and nature-spirits, the daughter of the Himalayas, and the personification of cosmic energy.

PE
In Voodoo, a small stone altar used in magickal ceremonies and sacrificial rituals.

PEGOMANCY
The art and practice of divination by bubbling fountains of water.

PEKKO
Finnish god of barley.

PEKO
Estonian fertility god whose sacred feast was celebrated on the first night of October.

PENDULUM
A divinatory device consisting of a small weight such as a piece of metal, a quartz crystal, a ring, or other heavy object suspended from a string or chain and used in dowsing, psychometry and radiesthesia as a diagnostic implement.

PENTACLE
(1) One of the four suits of the Minor Arcana of the Tarot. (2) In Witchcraft and ceremonial magick, a flat wood, wax, metal, or clay disc bearing the motif of the mystical five-pointed pentagram star and used in magickal ceremonies and spells to represent feminine energy and the ancient element of Earth.

PENTAGRAM
The symbol of the five-pointed star within a circle which represents the four ancient elements of Fire, Water, Air and Earth surmounted by the Spirit. The pentagram symbol is used by many Witches and magicians in spells and magickal ceremonies. As a Witches' Star (or Goblin's Cross as it was called by churchmen of the Middle Ages), the pentagram symbolizes human spiritual aspirations when it is used with its point facing upwards. When its point faces down, the pentagram becomes a symbol of negativity, black magick and Satanism.

PENTALPHA
A magickal design formed by interlacing five A's, and used in divination and the conjurations of spirits.

PERYTON
In Classical mythology and folk-legend, a winged, deer-like creature similar to the Greek Pegasus. It was known to feed on sailors and cast human shadows, a unique characteristic which led scholars to believe that the perytons were actually the malignant ghosts of wayfarers who had suffered tragic deaths far from home.

PESSOMANCY
The art and practice of divination by pebbles.

PHALLISM
The worship of the male sexual organ; sex-worship.

PHANTOM
An apparition or ghost.

PHILOSOPHERS' STONE
In alchemy, a mystical substance manufactured through long and complicated alchemical processes that was

believed to possess the power to perfect matter and turn other materials into gold when mixed with them.

PHILTRE
A love potion.

PHRENOLOGY
The psuedo-science, art and practice of interpreting a man or woman's character or mental capability by reading the conformation of the skull; head-reading.

PHURBU
A triangular wooden nail used by Tibetan lamas and sorcerers to drive off or impale demonic spirits.

PHYLACTERY
A small leather box containing strips of parchment inscribed with magickal symbols or words of power and worn or carried as an amulet.

PHYSIOGNOMY
The art and practice of personal character analysis by interpreting the physical appearance of the facial features; face-reading.

PILLYWIGGIN
In Brittish folklore, a diminutive fairy that inhabits the wildflowers found growing at the foot of oak trees.

PISCES
In astrology, the twelfth sign of the zodiac, also known as the sign of the Two Fish. Pisces is a water sign, and is ruled by the planets Jupiter and Neptune. Impractical, intuitive, shrewd, unstable, shy and refined describe the typical traits of a person born under the Piscean sign.

PIXY (also PIXIE)
In British folklore, a small and mischievous fairy-like spirit believed to be the soul of an unbaptized infant.

PK
Abbreviation for psychokinesis.

PLANCHETTE
In spiritualism, a triangular pointer that is used to spell out spirit-guided messages on a Ouija board when touched by the fingertips of one or more persons or mediums. With a pencil attached, the planchette can also be used as a device for automatic writing. (See also AUTOMATIC WRITING; OUIJA.)

PLASKY
See NOCNITSA

PLAT-EYE
In West Indian and southern United States folk belief, a demonic spiritual being that appears at night in the shape of a monstrous dog with glowing eyes of red fire.

PLUTO
In Roman mythology, the god of the dead and Lord of the Underworld, identified with the Greek god Hades; In astrology, the planetary ruler of the sign Scorpio.

PODOMANCY
The art and practice of divination by interpretation of the lines on the bottom of the feet, a method similar to palmistry.

POLTERGEIST
A ghost that manifests itself by loud noises, rappings, and even violent acts such as starting fires or mali-

ciously breaking household items. The word POLTER-GEIST stems from the German *polter* ("to make noise") and *geist* ("a spirit").

POLYTHEISM
The belief in or worship of more than one god.

POOKA
In Irish folklore, a nocturnal, shape-shifting hobgoblin that appears in the form of an animal, usually an ugly black horse. The pooka has been known to protect wild animals against evil spirits, do household or yard chores at night while people sleep, and give human beings the ability to understand animals' speech. The pooka is generally regarded as a harmless but mischievous being; however, it was greatly feared by the Druid priests of Ireland who believed that it was responsible for destroying or contaminating any crops not gathered by the last day of October, the ancient Celtic New Year known as Samhain.

POPPET
A specially prepared herb-stuffed cloth doll that is used in sympathetic magick rituals to represent the person at whom the spell is directed.

PORTENT
An omen or prophetic sign.

POSSESSION
In spiritualism, the phenomenon in which a spirit, either good or evil, takes control of a spiritualist medium in a state of trance during a seance. (See also DEMONIC POSSESSION.)

POTION
In Witchcraft, an herbal tea or brew used in a magickal or healing ritual.

PRACTICAL MAGICK
Witchcraft, folk-magick; magick that is concerned with things of the earth, harmony with Nature, seasons, and cycles. Unlike Ceremonial Magick which requires complicated rituals and elaborate (and often expensive) ritual tools and ceremonial clothing, practical magick is performed with the aid of simple, common implements.

PRANA
A powerful healing energy which emanates from the human body. It is controlled by the mind, possesses polarity, and has properties similar to other forms of energy but is a distinct force unto itself.

PRECOGNITION
In parapsychology, the paranormal or extrasensory perception of future events, usually through dreams or visions; psychic awareness of the future.

PREDICTION
A foretelling of the future by means of astrology, precognition, divination or omens.

PREMONITION
A psychic sense or intuitive feeling about future events before they happen; presage.

PRESAGE
An intuitive feeling that indicates or warns of a future occurrence; to predict the future or foretell an event before it happens.

PRESENTIMENT
A premonition.

PRIAPIC
A term used to describe deities possessing erect or exaggerated sexual organs. The Greek love god Eros, the Scandinavian fertility god Frey, and the Vodoun loa Ghede are several examples of priapic deities.

PRIAPUS
A faun-like nature god of gardens and fertility, whose sacrifice was the first fruits of the farm; a son of Aphrodite. In ancient Rome, figures of Priapus were used as magickal amulets to protect the wearer against the powers of the evil eye, and to insure the fertility of crops, animals and women.

PROPHECY
A prediction made by a Prophet.

PROPHESY
To predict the future or to speak as a Prophet.

PROPHET
A gifted person who speaks as the interpreter through whom a divinity expresses its will; a sooth-sayer or predictor; a person who receives symbolic spiritual messages from a god or goddess.

PROPHETESS
A female Prophet.

PSI
The phenomena of psychic power and extrasensory perception.

PSYCHE
The soul or spirit as distinguished from the physical body.

PSYCHIC
In parapsychology, a person responsive to psychic forces; one who possesses the gift of paranormal powers.

PSYCHISM
Extrasensory perception.

PSYCHOKINESIS
In parapsychology, the production of motion in inanimate objects by the exercise of paranormal mind powers.

PSYCHOMANCY
The art and practice of divination by men's souls, affections, wills, and religious or moral dispositions.

PSYCHOMETRY
In parapsychology, the art and practice of receiving psychic impressions of a person by holding a physical object that has been in their possession.

PSYCHOPLASM
Ectoplasm.

PUCK
In English folklore, a mischievous shape-shifting fairy-like creature, similar to a brownie or hobgoblin.

PYROMANCY
The art and practice of divination through the interpretation of the color, shape and intensity of a fire into

which sacred herbs, twigs or incense have been cast. Another method of pyromancy was to throw peas into a fire. If they burned quickly, it was interpreted as a favorable omen. When a sacrificial fire was used, the practice of divination was called empyromancy.

PYROSCOPY
See PYROMANCY.

QABBALAH
See KABBALAH.

QIQIRN
In Central Eskimo folklore, a supernatural creature that appears in the form of a huge, hairless dog, and causes men and animals to have fits.

QUADRUPEDALS
In astrology, the five zodiac signs represented by four-footed creatures: Aries, Capricorn, Leo, Sagittarius and Taurus.

QUADRUPLICITIES
In astrology, the division of the twelve zodiac signs into threefold classification of cardinal signs (Aries, Cancer, Capricorn, Libra), fixed signs (Aquarius, Leo, Scorpio, Taurus), and mutable signs (Gemini, Pisces, Sagittarius, Virgo).

QUDLIVUN
In Central Eskimo mythology, the happy spirit-land in the sky where souls of persons who have suffered in life or died young go to after death.

QUERENT
In astrology and divination, a man or woman who asks questions of the astrologer or fortune-teller.

QUETZALCOATL
Aztec god of fertility, wind and wisdom, personified as a feathered serpent and associated with the Morning Star.

QUINCUNX
In astrology, an aspect characterized by a 150 degree angle between planets

QUINTESSENCE

In ancient and medieval philosophy, the fifth and highest essence (after the four elements of fire, water, air and earth) also known as Aether or Spirit, and believed to be the substance of the heavenly bodies and latent in all things; in alchemy, the Philosopher's Stone.

QUIRINUS

A secondary Roman god of war and thunder, whose festival, the Quirinalia, was celebrated on the 17th of February.

RA
Sun god of ancient Egypt, identified as a god of birth and re-birth. He was worshipped at Heliopolis and was the main deity in the Ennead.

RADIESTHESIA
The technique of medical dowsing using the interpretations of a pendulum's motion to indicate the presence of a disease.

RAIDEN
In Japanese mythology, the flesh-eating god of thunder, also known as Kaminari Sama. He is a powerful deity, depicted as a demon with huge claws and a string of drums.

RAJA YOGA
A branch of yoga based on the Sutras of Patanjali that is devoted to the control of the mind and physical body.

RAKSHASAS
In Hindu folklore and mythology, hostile demigod demons who appear in either animal or human forms, haunt cemeteries and feed on human flesh and corpses.

REDCAP
In Scottish Border county folklore, a terrifying supernatural dwarf who dwells in abandoned castles where a murder or other act of violence has been committed. The redcap (also known as redcomb, dunter, bloodycap or powrie) is said to attack unsuspecting travelers and then dye his cap in the warm blood of his victims. According to legend, a mortal could defeat the redcap only by holding a Crucifix or cross-handled sword in front of its eyes. The creature would then vanish, leaving behind only a talon-like fingernail.

REINCARNATION
The repeated birth of the same soul in different physical bodies. Reincarnation is an ancient and mystical belief that is part of many religions, including Wicca, and is commonly associated with the concept of spiritual evolution.

RETRIBUTION
The reward or punishment given in a future life or incarnation based on the performance of good or evil in the present lifetime; karma. (See THREE-FOLD LAW.)

RETROCOGNITION
In parapsychology, the opposite of precognition; the paranormal ability to perceive events of the past.

RHABDOMANCY
The art and practice of divination by wand, rod or wooden stick. Some rhabdomancers draw omens by marking special divination sticks with symbols or names, casting them into a vessel, and then interpreting the first one drawn out. Another method is to cast the sticks into the air and then interpret the position in which they fall. (See also BELOMANCY; CLEROMANCY.)

RHAPSODOMANCY
The art and practice of divination by books of poetry or song lyrics. A book is opened to a page selected at random and the first line that comes to view is interpreted as prophetic. (See also BIBLIOMANCY.)

RHIANNON
Celtic/Welsh mother-goddess, originally called Rigatone (Great Queen) and identified with the Gaulish mare-goddess Epona. Rhiannon is represented in myth

riding a pale-white horse and carrying a magickal bag of abundance.

RIGHT-HAND PATH
The practice of white magick.

RING OF GYGES
In medieval sorcery, an invisibility ring made of fixed mercury, set with a stone from a lapwing's nest and engraved with magickal words or Biblical verses. It was believed that when it was worn on the finger, the wearer of the ring could make himself invisible or visible at will simply by turning the stone outward or inward.

RISHI
In Hindu mythology, a sage or holy man who possesses superhuman powers, and is regarded as being equal or often superior to the gods.

RISING SIGN
See ASCENDANT.

RITUAL
A religious or magickal ceremony characterized by symbolic attire and formalized behavior, and designed to produce desired effects such as spiritual illumination or "supernatural" power, or to invoke a specific deity.

RITUAL MAGICK
Ceremonial Magick.

ROADOMANCY
The art and practice of divination by interpretation of the stars.

RUDRA
The Vedic god of storms and "bringer of death" who inflicts, as well as heals, diseases in man.

RUNES

Letters of a secret magickal alphabet that spell words of power and are widely used in magick and divination. Runes can be written, painted or carved into ritual tools, magicians' robes, talismans, amulets, ceremonial jewelry and other things to charge the object with power. They also can be marked on flat wooden sticks or stones and used to divine future events or unknown circumstances. There are three main types of Runes: Anglo-Saxon, Germanic and Scandinavian. Their variations and subdivisions include the Druidic Ogam Bethluisnion, Egyptian hieroglyphics, Theban Script, Pictish, Celestial, Malachim and Passing the River.

RUSALKY

In Russian folklore, dangerous enchantress-fairies who inhabit rivers and lakes. They are said to appear in the guise of beautiful women, and seduce their human victims to a watery demise.

SABBAT
One of the eight Wiccan festivals; the gathering of Witches to celebrate at specific times of the year that mark transitions in the seasons. The four Grand Sabbats are: Candlemas, Beltane, Lammas and Samhain. The four Lesser Sabbats are: Spring Equinox, Summer Solstice, Autumn Equinox, and Winter Solstice which is also called Yule.

SACI
In Brazilian folklore and African-derived religious beliefs, a mischievous woodland spirit or nymph.

SACRIFICE
In Voodoo and other primitive religions, the ritual slaughter of an animal as an offering to a deity for fertility, magickal power, protection, etc. In many ancient cultures, including the Celtic Druids, both animals and humans were sacrificed as ritual offerings to appease the gods.

SAGA
A term used in the Middle Ages for a fortune-teller.

SAGITTARIUS
In astrology, the ninth sign of the zodiac, symbolized by the archer. Sagittarius is a fire sign, and is ruled by the planet Jupiter. Independence and outspokenness are typical Sagittarian traits.

SAINT AGNES' EVE
The night of January 20th, when, according to folklegend, an unmarried woman will see her future husband or lover in a dream. Saint Agnes' Eve (named after the Roman Catholic child martyr who was beheaded in 304 A.D. for refusing to marry) was also the time when

medieval Witches cast love spells and prepared love philtres and charms.

SAINT JOHN'S EVE

The night before Midsummer's Day. Saint John's Eve (June 23rd) is a traditional time for Witches to gather herbs for spells and potions, for it is believed that the magickal properties of plants are the greatest on this night. In many parts of Scandinavia, bonfires were lit at crossroads on Saint John's Eve to scare away the dark forces of trolls and evil ghosts. In the Middle Ages, Saint John's Wort was hung on doors and windows on Saint John's Eve to keep the Devil away, and worn around the necks of children and animals to protect them from illness during the entire year. Countless other folk customs and superstitions are associated with Saint John's Eve.

St. JOHN'S WORT

A healing herb associated with magick and Witchcraft. St. John's wort, so called because it was gathered on St. John's Eve to ward off evil spirits, was hung in doors and windows during the Middle Ages to protect against demonic influences, and is a common herb used in exorcisms and anti-sorcery charms.

SALAMANDER

The elemental spirit of Fire.

SALUS

In Roman mythology, a goddess of health, prosperity and well-being; identified with the Greek goddess Hygeia.

SALVANELLI

In Italian folklore, playful tree-dwelling sprites who dress in worn, red overalls or jerkins, and amuse themselves by stealing milk from farmers and riding their horses to exhaustion.

SAMBO-KOJIN
In Japanese folk belief, a deity who protects and watches over the kitchen. He is depicted as a triple-faced man with four hands.

SAMHAIN
One of the four Grand Sabbats, also known as Halloween, and celebrated on October 31st. Samhain is the most important of all the Witches' Sabbats. It is the ancient Celtic/Druid New Year, and also the time when spirits of deceased loved ones and friends are honored. At one time in history, many believed that it was the night when the dead returned to walk among the living. The divinatory arts of scrying and runecasting are Samhain traditions among many Wiccans.

SANTERA
A priestess of Santeria.

SANTERIA
An Afro-Cuban earth religion, similar to Voodoo, which blends together primitive African magic and beliefs with Catholic Church traditions. Santeria, which originated in Cuba, has its roots in Nature, and is based on the concepts of *ashe* (divine power) and *ebbo* (sacrifice). The religion was brought to Cuba over four centuries ago by the Yoruba slaves from West Africa. The deities (*orisha*) worshipped by the priests and priestesses of Santeria are associated with the various forces of Nature and identified with Catholic saints. The term Santeria derives from the Spanish word *santo* (saint) and literally means "the worship of saints." It is estimated that there are over 100 million practitioners of Santeria in Latin America and the United States.

SANTERO
A priest of Santeria.

SARASVATI
A Vedic river goddess, worshipped for her purifying and fertilizing powers. In later mythology, Sarasvati was regarded as the goddess of wisdom and eloquence, and consort of the god Brahma.

SARAYEYEOS
In the religion of Santeria, the ritual rubbing of the body with fruits, bones, or sacrificial animals to cleanse spiritual impurities and remove negative influences from an individual by transferring his or her problems or illness onto the objects used.

SATAN
In Christianity, the enemy of God and personification of supreme evil who was envisaged as a bearded man with horns and a serpent's tail who tempts mortals with sin and bargains for human souls. He is also known as the Devil, Lucifer, Beelzebub, Old Scratch, the Lord of Hell, the Prince of Darkness, and hundreds of other names.

SATANIC MASS
See BLACK MASS.

SATANISM
The worship of Satan, the cult of devil-worship.

SATIRE
In Old Irish mythology and folk legend, a magickal rhyming curse that was believed to possess the power to bring illness or death to any enemy when recited.

SATURN
Roman god of the harvest, identified with the Greek god Cronus; In astrology, the planetary ruler of the zodiac signs Capricorn and Aquarius.

SATYR
In Greek mythology, an anthropomorphic woodland deity having the pointed ears, legs and short horns of a goat.

SCEPTER
A wand used in magickal ceremonies and rituals.

SCIOMANCY
The art and practice of divination by the interpretation of shadows.

SCORPIO
In astrology, the eighth sign of the zodiac, symbolized by the scorpion. Scorpio is a water sign, and is ruled by the planets Mars and Pluto. Intelligence, sensitivity, manipulation, secretiveness and vindictiveness are typical Scorpion traits.

SCRYING
The art and practice of interpreting the future, past, or present from images seen while gazing into a crystal ball, candle flame, pool of water, or gazing mirror; crystal-gazing; mirror-gazing.

SEAL OF SOLOMON
A hexagram consisting of two interlocking triangles, one facing up and the other facing down. It symbolizes the human soul and is used by many Witches and magicians in spells and rituals involving spirit communication, wisdom, purification and/or the strengthening of psychic powers.

SEAMAIDEN
A sea-nymph or mermaid.

SEANCE
In spiritualism, a gathering of persons to contact and receive messages from discarnate beings or spirits of the dead. A seance is held in the dark or by candlelight at a table where all persons attending are seated with hands joined together to form a circle. At all seances, at least one medium must be present to serve as a channel for communications.

SECOND SIGHT
Clairvoyance.

SEER
A male clairvoyant; one who is gifted with the power of second sight.

SEERESS
A female clairvoyant.

SEIDE
Sacred human or animal-shaped stones used by the Lapps as magickal divination stones and good luck amulets.

SEKHMET
Ancient Egyptian war-goddess and consort of the god Ptah. She is depicted as a woman with the head of a lion and is the Egyptian counterpart of the Hindu goddess Shakti.

SELENE
The Greek moon-goddess in her waxing aspect. In her waning aspect, she is called Hecate.

SENDING
In Icelandic folk belief, an evil ghost created by black magick from a human bone, and used by a sorcerer to murder enemies. The sending appears as a black, smoky shadow with a white spot in the center. It is said that the only way to destroy a sending is to stab its white spot with a steel blade, turning it back into a harmless bone.

SEPHIROT
In the Kabbalah, the ten emanations of God on the Tree of Life which represent different levels of spiritual reality in man and the cosmos, and are meditated upon as the central part of Kabbalistic doctrine. The ten Sephirot consist of: Crown, Wisdom, Intelligence, Love, Justice, Beauty, Firmness, Splendor, Foundation, and Kingdom.

SESHA
In Hindu mythology, the thousand-headed serpent who supports the world and causes earthquakes when he shakes one of his heads.

SET
Ancient Egyptian god of darkness and black magick, and the personification of evil. He is the Egyptian counterpart of the Greek god Typhon. (Also spelled SETH.)

SEX MAGICK
A potent form of magick that uses the sexual experience and orgasm to generate the power to work magick.

SHADE
A ghost or apparition.

SHAMAN
A priest, priestess, medicine-man, spirit-healer or other person of psychic sensitivity who possesses arcane knowledge and the ability to enter a trance state, control the spirit forces, and communicate with the divine through the ritual use of drumming and various states of consciousness.

SHAMASH
Babylonian sun-god, brother of the goddess Ishtar, and a deity associated with oracles of prophecy. He is identified with the Sumerian god Utu and the Greek god Apollo.

SHAPE-SHIFTER
One who possesses the supernatural ability to transform into animals or mythic creatures. See also ZOO-MORPHISM.

SHEITAN
Among the Moslems, an evil spirit or fiend.

SHEW-STONE
A flat, circular, black stone with a highly polished surface used in the same manner as a crystal ball to divine the future or the past.

SIDEROMANCY
The art and practice of divination by throwing an odd number of straws upon a red-hot iron and drawing omens from the twisting and bending of the burning straws, the intensity of the flames and/or the course of the smoke.

SIDHE
In Irish folklore, a supernatural fairy-like creature.

SIGIL
In Ceremonial Magick, an image that symbolizes a specific spirit, deity, angel or supernatural being, and is used in evocations and invocations to summon the entity which it represents. See also VEVES.

SIGN
An omen; in astrology, the twelve divisions of the zodiac, each named for a constellation or represented by a symbol. The twelve signs of the zodiac are: Aries, Taurus, Gemini, Cancer, Leo, Virgo, Libra, Scorpio, Sagittarius, Capricorn, Aquarius and Pisces.

SIGNIFICATOR
In cartomancy, a specific card that is used to represent the man or woman whose fortune is being told.

SILENUS
(1) in Greek mythology, the satyr-like god of forests and springs, and foster father of Bacchus. (2) any of various minor woodland deities or spirits and companions of Dionysus, the Greek god of wine.

SIMBI
In Voodoo, a Petro loa known as the Patron of Magickal Powders. He is believed to inhibit mango and calabash trees. Tuesday is his sacred day.

SIMURG
A gigantic, bejeweled bird which, according to Persian mythology and folk-legend, guarded royalty and the families of Persian heroes. Its feathers possessed great healing powers and could endow a mortal man with superhuman strength.

SIXTH SENSE
Extrasensory perception.

SKOGSRA
In Swedish folklore, shape-shifting wood elves who often assume the form of great horned owls.

SKYCLAD
A Wiccan word meaning "in the nude"; ritual nudity.

SMUDGING
The burning of incense or herbs to drive away negative forces and to purify the space in which white magick is to be performed.

SOBO
In Voodoo, a Rada loa who controls thunder and lightning, and whose sacred symbol is the ram. The Voudounist believe that Sobo forges sacred thunderstones (pre-Columbian axe-heads) by hurling a thunderbolt to the Earth, striking a rock outcropping and casting a stone to the floor of the valley. Before a houngan may touch it with his hands, the thunderstone must lie there for a year and one day.

SOLISTRY
The art and practice of divination by reading the lines and markings on the soles of the feet. This form of divination is also known as podomancy, and was a common practice among the ancient Chinese, Persians and Indians.

SOLITARY
A Witch who practices magick without belonging to a coven.

SOMNUS
In Roman mythology, the god of sleep and dreams; identified with the Greek god Hypnos. (Compare with MORPHEUS.)

SOOTHSAYER
A clairvoyant; one who possesses the ability to divine future events.

SORCERER
A male practitioner of sorcery.

SORCERESS
A female practitioner of sorcery.

SORCERY
The use of supernatural power for either material gain or to harm others, often through the assistance of evil spirits or demons; black magick.

SORTILEGE
The art and practice of divination by the casting or drawing of lots.

SORTITION
The art and practice of divination by casting lots to determine the answer of a previously thought-of question. Also known as sortilege and lot-casting.

SPAGYRIC ART
Alchemy.

SPATALAMANCY
The art and practice of divination by interpretation of skins, bones and excrements.

SPECTER
A term used in spiritualism to describe an apparition or ghost.

SPECULUM
A crystal ball or other object possessing a shiny, reflective surface and used in scrying as an object to focus one's gaze in entering a state of trance-consciousness.

SPELL
An incantational formula; a non-religious magickal ritual performed by a Witch, wizard or magician for either good or evil.

SPELLCASTER
A Witch, sorcerer or magician; one who casts spells.

SPIRIT
The vital principle, divine essence or animating force within all living persons; a discarnate entity, ghost or apparition.

SPIRITISM
Spiritualism.

SPIRITUALISM
The belief that the spirits of the deceased are able to communicate with the living through a medium in a state of trance, or by other means.

SPIRITUALIST
A medium who channels spirits of the dead.

SPODOMANCY
The art and practice of divination by interpretation of cinders or soot taken from a sacrificial fire.

SPRING EQUINOX
One of the four Lesser Sabbats celebrated by Witches; the vernal equinox. See OSTARA.

SPRITE
An elf, fairy, nymph or pixie; an archaic word used to describe a ghost or specter.

STAREOMANCY
The art and practice of divination by the elements.

STARGAZER
One who practices astrology; an astrologer.

STERNOMANCY
The art and practice of divination by interpretation of the breastbone.

STICHOMANCY
See BIBLIOMANCY.

STRIX
A term used in the Middle Ages for a sorceress. (Plural: STRIGES.)

SUCCUBUS
In medieval folklore, a demon or evil spirit that takes on the shape of a beautiful woman and seduces men as they sleep in order to possess their souls. The male equivalent of the succubus is the incubus.

SUFFUMIGATIONS
In Witchcraft and sorcery, magickal incenses made from herbs, and burned to attract spirits and enable them to materialize.

SUFISM
A sect of Islamic mysticism and Tantric Goddess/female-worship dating from the Eighth Century A.D. and developed chiefly in the country of Persia (now Iran).

SUKYA
A shaman or sorcerer in the Miskito and Sumi Indian tribes of Nicaragua and northeastern Honduras.

SUMMER SOLSTICE
One of the four Lesser Sabbats celebrated by Witches. The Summer Solstice, also known as the Midsummer Festival, marks the longest day of the year when the sun is at its zenith, and is the traditional time when Witches harvest magickal herbs for spells and potions, for it is believed that the innate power of herbs are strongest on this day. In certain Wiccan traditions, the Summer Solstice symbolizes the end of the reign of the Oak-King who is now replaced by his successor the Holly-King who will rule until the Sabbat of Yule, which marks the shortest day of the year.

SUN
In astrology, the planetary ruler of the zodiac sign Leo.

SUN SIGN
In astrology, the sign of the zodiac which an individual is born under; the birth-sign.

SURYA
The Hindu sun god.

SWASTIKA
An ancient cosmic or religious symbol formed by a Greek cross with the ends of the arms bent at right

angles in either a clockwise or counterclockwise direction. Before being adopted in 1935 as the infamous official emblem of Nazi Germany, the swastika was used as a sacred religious symbol and/or good luck talisman in pre-Christian Europe and in many other cultures across the world including the Orientals, Egyptians, and the Indian tribes of North, Central and South America. The word swastika stems from the Sanskrit SVASTIKA, meaning a "sign of good luck." There are over 1200 known swastika designs, the oldest dating back to 12,000 B.C.

SWORDS
One of the four suits of the Minor Arcana of the Tarot.

SYCOMANCY
The art and practice of divination by figs.

SYLPHS
Elemental spirits of Air.

SYLVANUS
In Roman mythology, the god of forests, fields and herding, depicted as a bearded satyr.

SYMPATHETIC MAGICK
See IMAGE MAGICK

TALISMAN

A man-made object of any shape or material charged with magickal properties to bring good luck, fertility and ward off evil. To formally charge a talisman with power, it must first be inscribed and then consecrated. Inscribing the talisman with a sun sign, moon sign, birthdate, Runic name or other magickal symbol personalizes it and gives it purpose.

TANE

Polynesian sky-god and lord of fertility who was believed to have created the first man out of red clay.

TANGAROA

In Polynesian mythology, the god of the sea, and patron of all fishermen.

TANTRA

(1) one of a comparatively recent class of approximately 64 Buddhist or Hindu written scriptures concerned with sex-magick, mysticism, and the postures of love. (2) a form of Kundalini yoga in which a woman's divine spiritual energy is aroused and a man's realization of the divinity is achieved through ceremonial emotional and sexual union without male orgasm.

TANTRISM

A religious system of yoni-worship or female-centered sex-worship associated with the Hindu religious texts known as the Tantras. One of the prayer mantras (spoken formulas incorporating "words of power") most sacred in Tantrism is *om mani padme hum* which translates to: "So be it! O jewel (symbol of the male penis) in the lotus (symbol of the female vulva). Amen" and refers to the sexual union of the god Shiva and the goddess Shakti. (See also *TANTRA*)

TAROT
A deck of 78 cards used for reading the past, the future and fortune. It is divided into two parts: the Minor Arcana and the Major Arcana. The Minor Arcana consists of 56 divinatory cards divided into four suits of 14 cards each: Swords, Pentacles, Wands and Cups. The Major Arcana consists of 22 highly symbolic trump cards with colorful allegorical figures. The various methods of Tarot card reading include the Celtic Cross method, the Golden Dawn method (modified by Aleister Crowley) and the Oracles of Julia Orsini, which is an ancient French method that uses a significator card plus 42 other cards.

TASE
In Burmese folk belief, one of a group of evil, disembodied spirits who appear in the form of animals or as grotesque, bloodthirsty giants with long, slimy tongues.

TASSEOGRAPHY
The art and practice of divination by interpretation of the symbolic patterns made by tea leaves in a cup; tea-leaf reading. This form of divination is associated mainly with Gypsy fortune-tellers.

TATZLWURM
In Swiss and Austrian folklore, winged fire-breathing dragons which dwell in high mountains and feed upon stray cattle and lost children.

TAURUS
In astrology, the second sign of the zodiac, symbolized by the bull. Taurus is an earth sign, and is ruled by the planet Venus. Stubbornness, loyalty, stability and patience are typical Taurean traits.

TELEKINESIS
In parapsychology, the spontaneous movement of physical objects by scientifically unknown or inexplicable means, as by the exercise of paranormal powers.

TELEPATHY
In parapsychology, the transfer of thoughts from one mind into another; mind-to-mind communication; thought reading. Also called Mental Telepathy.

TELEPLASM
See ECTOPLASM.

TELEPORTATION
In parapsychology, the ability to transport physical objects or human beings through space without mechanical or physical means.

TENGU
In Japanese folk belief, a race of winged, gnome-like beings revered for their mastery of the martial arts and of the warrior's spirit. It was regarded as a blessing for any mortal to walk among the Tengu, and under their tutelage, a person could develop great physical power.

TEPHRAMANCY
The art and practice of drawing omens from the ashes of a burned tree trunk.

THANATOS
Greek god of death whose Roman counterpart was the god Mors.

THEISM
Belief in the existence of gods or goddesses.

THEOMANCY
The art and practice of divination by consultation of spirits or divine beings.

THERIOMANCY
The art and practice of divination by beasts.

THERIOMORPHISM
Gods in animal form.

THIRD EYE
In Kundalini yoga, the sixth of the seven chakras known as the Ajna ·chakra; the human body's highest source of power, supernormal sight and clairvoyant vision. The third eye is invisible and is said to be located above the eyebrows in the middle of the forehead.

THOR
Scandinavian sky-god, master of thunderbolts, son of Odin, and patron god of farmers and sailors. He is depicted as a strong but friendly man with wild hair and a long, red beard. His sacred symbol is the hammer.

THOTH
Ancient Egyptian god of the moon, wisdom, magick, arts and science. He was also known as the scribe of the gods, and is depicted as an ibis, an ibis-headed man, and also as an ape. The truth-goddess Maat was his consort and the first month of the Egyptian year was named after him.

THREE-FOLD LAW
In Wicca, the belief that if one does good, he or she will get it back threefold in the same lifetime. Whatever harm one does to others is also returned threefold. (Also known as Triple Karma.)

THUNOR
Pagan-Germanic god of thunder and lightning, and a deity associated with fertility. Thursday is his sacred day of the week.

THURIBLE
In Witchcraft and Wicca, a shallow, three-legged dish used in magickal workings as an incense burner.

TIKI
A human-shaped amulet made of wood and mother of pearl, and used to symbolize the creative power of the Polynesian sky-god Tane.

TI KITA
In Voodoo, a powerful and much feared female Petro loa associated with the cult of magick and the dead.

TIWAZ
Pagan-Germanic sky-god and consort of Frija.

TLAZOLTEOTL
Central American earth-goddess associated with fertility and love. She is also known as the Mother of All Gods.

T.M.
Transcendental Meditation.

TORNAK
In Central Eskimo religion, the guardian spirit of a shaman.

TRAITEURS
Folk doctors who treat snakebites, illnesses and spells with old-fashioned herbal and occult remedies.

TRANCE
In spiritualism, a state in which a medium loses consciousness, thus permitting spirits to enter and speak or act through the physical body of the trance medium.

TRANSCENDENTAL MEDITATION
A form of meditation requiring total relaxation and concentration upon a personal secret mantra to heighten self-awareness and tranquility.

TRANSFIGURATION
In spiritualism, the phenomenon of a trance-medium's facial transformation into the physical characteristics and mannerisms of the communicating spirit.

TRANSIT
In astrology, the movement of a planet through a house or sign.

TRANSMIGRATION
Metempsychosis; the passing of a soul after death into a different physical body, either human or animal.

TREE OF LIFE
A Kabbalistic diagram showing the ten Sephirot (emanations of God) and their relationship to each other. See also KABBALAH; SEPHIROT.

TRIANGLE
A symbol of finite manifestation in Western magick, used in rituals to evoke spirits when the seal or sign of the entity to be summoned is placed in the center of the triangle. The triangle, equivalent to the number three (a powerful magickal number) is also a symbol of the Triple Goddess: Maiden, Mother, Crone. Inverted, it represents the male principle.

TRICK

In Trinidad and southern United States folk magick, a magickal charm bag, variously known as a tricken bag, mojo bag, hoodoo hand, gris-gris, etc. When used in black magick for evil purposes, the trick is called a root bag or fingers-of-death.

TRIDENT

(1) in Paganism, a sacred triple-phallus symbol displayed by any male deity whose function is to sexually unite with the Triple Goddess. (2) the triple-pronged spear carried by the mythological sea-gods Neptune and Poseidon.

TRINE

In astrology, the aspect of two planets when 120 degrees apart.

TRIPLE GODDESS

A Goddess trinity having three different aspects and three different names. The Moon Mother is worshipped as a Triple Goddess whose sacred symbol is the crescent moon. Her three Goddess aspects correspond to the three lunar phases. In her waxing phase, she is the maiden. In her full moon phase, she is the mother. In her waning or dark moon phase, she is the crone of wisdom, death and darkness. In Norse mythos, the Triple Goddess trinity is: Freya (goddess of love and beauty), Frigga (mother-goddess) and Hel (queen of death and ruler of the underworld). The multiple aspects of the Celtic goddess Morrigan are: Macha, Badb and Neman. Even Mary of the Christian mythos is as much a trinity as any ancient Pagan goddess for she embodies the attributes found in female deities of other cultures: Virgin, Mother and Saint. There are also male God trinities such as the Hindu trimurti of Brahma,

Vishnu and Shiva; the Greek sun-god triad of Apollo, Helios and Phoebus; and the well-known Christian union of three divine figures, the Father, Son and Holy Ghost, in one godhead.

TROLL
In Scandinavian folklore, a friendly or mischievous supernatural being or elemental spirit portrayed as a dwarfish creature or a gigantic ogre. The small trolls were said to be wonderful and skillful craftsmen who lived under bridges, in hills or in dark caves, and exploded if the light of the sun touched their faces. The huge trolls possessed great strength, hunted in forests, and lived in castles where they guarded secret treasure.

TRUE MAGICK
Magick that is performed for good purposes such as to heal or help others; white magick; the opposite of black magick.

TUPHRAMANCY
The art and practice of divination by the interpretation of ashes.

TYPOMANCY
The art and practice of divination by the coagulation of cheese.

TYPTOLOGY
In spiritualism, the act of receiving psychic messages through table-turning, a method of spirit-communication in which a spirit raps systematically on a levitating table during a seance.

UDO
The Sumu Indian moon god.

U.F.O.
An Unidentified Flying Object.

UFOLOGIST
A person who studies U.F.O. phenomena.

UFOLOGY
The study of Unidentified Flying Objects; the research and investigation of space aliens and contact cases involving alleged encounters with aliens.

UHEPONO
In Zuni Indian mythology, an underworld giant with wooly skin, saucer-like eyes, and the arms and legs of a man.

UKKO
In Finnish mythology, the god of thunder clouds and rain.

UKUPANIPO
The Hawaiian shark-god.

UMBRAL ECLIPSE
In astrology, a lunar eclipse.

UNCROSSING RITUAL
In Ceremonial Magick and Wicca, a ritual designed to break the power of negative spells, black magick or evil influences.

UNCTION
The act of anointing with an oil or an herbal ointment as part of a consecration, magickal ceremony or healing ritual.

UNDERWORLD

In various ancient mythologies, a region, realm or dwelling place conceived to be below the surface of the Earth and separate from the world of the living where the souls of the deceased went after death; the world of the dead.

UNDINES

Female elemental spirits of water. Also known as nymphs, mermaids, mermen, nereids and oceanides.

UNGUENT

A special ointment or salve used by Witches to promote healing and to induce astral projections and psychic dreams. Also known as flying ointment and sorcerers' grease. In the Middle Ages, unguents containing various hallucinogenic ingredients were believed to give a Witch the powers of flight, invisibility and transformation.

UNICORN

A fabled creature in folk-legend and heraldry, represented as a gentle, horse-like beast with a single spiraled horn extending from its forehead, and often with a lion's tail and a goat's beard. The unicorn symbolized chastity, virginity, fierceness, and the power of love, and it was said that only the touch of a virgin could tame it. The horn of the unicorn (which has a white base, a black middle, and a red tip) was regarded to be extremely magickal, and it was believed to possess the powers to detect poisons and to make water pure, among other things. At one time the unicorn was believed to be a native of India, later of Africa.

URANUS

(1) Ancient Greek god known as Father Sky. He was the consort of the goddess Gaea, and personified the heav-

ens. (2) In astrology, one of the planetary rulers of the zodiac sign Aquarius.

URIM AND THUMMIM
Sacred lots used for divination or reading the oracles, and carried inside the breastplate of the High Priests of ancient Israel.

USHAS
In Vedic mythology, the goddess of dawn.

VAMPIRE

In folklore, a bloodsucking demon believed to be the reanimated corpse of a person who himself was bitten by a vampire. Vampires are said to possess the supernatural power to transform into bats or mist and are capable of making themselves invisible at will.

VAMPIRISM

The practice of drinking human blood.

VAYU

In Vedic mythology, the god of the wind and atmosphere; associated with Indra and represented by the antelope.

VELADA

Among the Mazatec Indians of Mexico, a sacred Shamanistic healing ritual involving psychedelic mushrooms.

VENEFICA

A term used in the Middle Ages for a Witch who uses magickal poisons and philtres.

VENUS

Roman and Neo-Pagan goddess of love and beauty; the personification of sexuality, fertility, prosperity and good fortune. She is the Roman counterpart of the Greek love-goddess Aphrodite. In astrology, the planetary ruler of the zodiac signs Taurus and Libra.

VERNAL EQUINOX

The Spring Equinox. See OSTARA.

VERVAIN

A spiky wayside plant with purplish-blue flowers and a magickal, mystical past. Vervain has been associated with Witches, sorcerers and magick since the beginning of history. In ancient times, the plant was bruised and worn as a charm against venomous bites and headaches. It was also believed to possess the power to cure grief. Today, vervain is used mainly in sleep potions, anti-sorcery spells and love magick.

VESTA
Roman goddess of the hearth whose temple was lit by a sacred fire tended by six virgin priestesses known as the Vestal Virgins.

VETALA
In Hindu folklore and mythology, a demonic spirit which inhabits cemeteries and animates the bodies of the dead.

VEVES
In Voodoo, intricate symbolic emblems that are drawn on the ground with flour or ashes to invoke the various loas, or Voodoo deities, which they represent.

VILA
In southern Slavic folklore, a dancing nymph who inhabits forests, fields, lakes and streams.

VIRGO
In astrology, the sixth sign of the zodiac, also known as the Virgin. Virgo is an earth sign, and is ruled by the planet Mercury. The typical Virgo person is romantic, generous, efficient, analytical, and a perfectionist.

VISHNU
In Hinduism, the chief deity worshipped by the Vaishnava, and one of the three Supreme Gods in the trinity including also Shiva and Brahma.

VISION
An altered state of consciousness in which a sacred or prophetic image is perceived; a mental image that appears in a dream, while in a trance, or while scrying.

VISIONARY
One who is gifted with paranormal vision.

VISUALIZATION
In magick, the process of forming mental images of needed goals during rituals and spellcasting. Also called Creative Visualization and Magickal Visualization.

VITKA
Rune-mistress; a Pagan priestess or seeress who divines the future by casting runestones into a circle drawn on the ground and interpreting the patterns formed by the stones.

VODUN
Same as Voodoo.

VOODOO
A very old and primitive system of both black and white magick, deriving from a background of African theology and ceremonialism. It is characterized by fetish-worship, animal sacrifices, frenzied drum dances, spirit possession and zombies. Voodoo is a complex of Catholic and African religious beliefs and rituals, establishing a vital link between the material world and the world of spirit, and governing in large measure the life of the Haitian peasantry. The word derives from the West African VODUN, meaning a "spirit" or "a god."

VOODOOISM
The practice of Voodoo as well as the view of life and death embodied in the Voodoo religion.

VOYANCE
In parapsychology, extrasensory perception or paranormal vision; psychic ability; psi.

WAKANDA
A Sioux Indian word meaning "supernatural power".

WALPURGISNACHT
May Eve, April 30th. (see BELTANE)

WAND
In Ceremonial Magick and Witchcraft, a wooden stick used to trace circles, draw magickal symbols on the ground, direct energy and stir cauldron brews; any stick, baton or rod used by a diviner or conjurer. The wand is the emblem of power, represents the element Fire (Air in Ceremonial Magick), and is sacred to the Pagan deities.

WANDS
One of the four suits of the Minor Arcana of the Tarot, ascribed to the element of Air.

WANGA
In Haitian Voodoo, a charm that works black magick.

WARLOCK
A word stemming from the Old English WAERLOGA meaning an "oath-breaker" and used derogatorily by the Church as a name for a male Witch. However, in Witchcraft and Wicca, the word warlock is seldom, if ever, used. Both male and female practitioners of the Craft are called Witches.

WATER
One of the four alchemical elements. The spirits of Water are known as undines.

WATER SIGNS
In astrology, the signs of the zodiac attributed to the ancient element of water: Cancer, Pisces and Scorpio.

WATER WITCH
A nickname used to describe a man or woman who uses a divining rod to locate underground water; a dowser.

WEATHERWORKING
The art and practice of controlling atmospheric conditions by means of magick, prayer or supernatural power; magickal control of the weather; rain-making. A medieval Witch's cauldron spell to raise tempests, a magician's incantation to summon the wind, rain-attracting lava stone amulets and Native American rain dances to promote rain are just a few examples of weatherworking.

WEREWOLF
In occult folklore, a human being believed to be physically transformed into a wolf or wolf-like creature by means of supernatural power or black magick; a lycanthrope.

WEZA
Burmese necromancers.

WHITE-HANDLED KNIFE
See BOLLINE.

WHITE MAGICK
The opposite of black magick; positive magick that is practiced only for good purposes or as a counter to evil. Love spells, healing rituals and luck-attracting amulets are several examples of white magick. Also known as true magick.

WICCA
An alternative name for modern Witchcraft; a Neo-Pagan nature religion with spiritual roots in Shaman-

ism, having one main tenet: the Wiccan Rede. The Goddess and Her consort the Horned God are the two main deities honored and worshipped in Wiccan rites. Their names vary from one Wiccan tradition to the next. Wicca includes the practice of various forms of white magick, as well as rites to attune oneself with the natural rhythm of life forces marked by the phases of the moon and the seasons.

WICCAN
A follower of Wicca.

WICCANING
A Wiccan birth rite by which a baby is given a name by its parents, anointed on the forehead with salted water by a coven Priestess, and then passed through the smoke of incense by its mother as a gesture of purification.

WICCAN REDE
A simple and benevolent moral code of Wiccans that is as follows: "An it harm none, do what thou wilt."

WICHTLEIN
In German folklore, dwarf-like supernatural beings who dwell in mines. The wichtlein have been known to warn humans of impending mine disasters and to cause showers of rocks to rain down on miners as a sign of abundant ore. Mine-dwelling dwarfs like the wichtlein are common in most European folklore and legend: in the coal mines of Wales, these small creatures were known as coblynau; in the tin mines of Cornwall they were called knockers; and in the silver mines of Bohemia they were named haus-schmiedlein.

WIDDERSHINS
A Wiccan word meaning counter-clockwise. This motion symbolizes negative magickal purposes and is mainly used to uncast the circle at the end of a ritual.

WINDIGO
In Algonquin Indian mythology and folk belief, an evil, ogre-like creature that lives in forests and devours its human victims.

WINTER SOLSTICE SABBAT
See YULE.

WINTI-MAN
A Dutch Guiana magician or priest who worships the African gods.

WITCH
A person, male or female, who practices Witchcraft; one who worships the gods of the Old Religion; a Wiccan.

WITCH BALL
A mirror-like ball of silver glass hung in a dark corner or suspended in a window to avert the harmful influences of the evil eye either by attracting to itself the negative influences that would otherwise have fallen upon the household, or by casting back the negative influence upon the person who sent it forth.

WITCHCRAFT
The Old Religion; the Craft of the Wise; the practice of folk-religion that combines magick, nature-worship, divination and herbalism with bits and pieces of various pre-Christian religious beliefs such as those of the Druids and the ancient Egyptians. In 16th century Europe, organized religion felt that the ways of the Old Religion

were a threat to their belief system and as a result, the practice of Witchcraft in England was made an illegal offense in the year 1541. In 1604, a law decreeing capital punishment for Witches was adopted and the pulpit became a platform for the denunciation and extermination of anyone suspected of worshipping the old gods. Forty years later, the thirteen colonies in America also made Witchcraft a crime punishable by death. By the end of the 17th century, Witches were in hiding and the Old Religion had become a secret underground religion after an estimated one million Europeans had been put to death and more than thirty condemned at Salem, Massachusetts, in the name of Christianity. Not until 1951 were the laws against Witchcraft in England finally repealed.

WITCH DOCTOR
Among the primitive cultures in Africa, Australia, Central America, Haiti, Melanesia, Polynesia and South America, a practitioner of magick who uses spells and charms to cure the ill and exorcise evil spirits from possessed persons and places.

WITCH-DRAUGHT
In medieval Witchcraft and sorcery, a magickal potion, brew, or philtre used to control or manipulate the emotions and/or thoughts of others.

WITCHES' LADDER
In sorcery, a knotted triple cord, string or rope, usually with a feather in each knot, used by sorcerers as a powerful magickal charm to bring nightmares, misfortune, illness or death to enemies. Also called a Witches' garland.

WITCHES' SABBAT
See *SABBAT*

WITCHLING
The child of a Witch.

WIVERN
In folklore and heraldry, a two-legged dragon with wings and a barbed and knotted tail. Also spelled wyvern.

WIZARD
A male Witch, adept, sage or magician skilled in summoning supernatural powers. The word derives from the Middle English WIS, meaning "wise."

WIZARDRY
The art, skill or practice of a wizard.

WODEN
Pagan-Germanic god of war, skald-craft (poetry), prophecy and magick, whose sacred day of the week was Wednesday. Woden is also known as the Lord of the Dead, the primeval runemaster and the god of shape-shifting. Mythology shows Woden to be the highest deity of the German pantheon. The name Woden is the English form of the name ultimately derived from a Proto-Germanic form Wodh-an-az, meaning, "the master of inspired psychic activity." As a Neo-Pagan deity, he is worshipped mainly by Wiccans of the Saxon tradition, and is often identified with the Scandinavian god Odin, the mightiest of the Teutonic deities.

WORDS OF POWER
In Ceremonial Magick, conjurations and invocations used in rituals and ceremonies, and often consisting of Jewish god-names.

WORTCUNNING
In Witchcraft and Wicca, the use of and knowledge of the secret healing and magickal properties of herbs.

WRAITH
The apparition of a living person; the ghost of a dead person. See DOPPELGANGER, FETCH, GHOST, SPECTER.

WYVERN
See WIVERN.

XENOGLOSSY
In spiritualism and parapsychology, the act of speaking-in-tongues. Also known as xenoglossis and xeno-glossisia.

XEVIOSO
In Voodoo, Haitian and Dahomean gods of thunder and the sea.

XOCHIQUETZAL
Central American goddess of flowers.

XYLOMANCY
The art and practice of drawing omens from twigs or pieces of wood by interpreting their shapes and formations, or by the way they burn when placed upon a fire.

YAKA
In Vedda (Ceylon) religion and folk belief, the stone-throwing spirit of a dead person. (Compare with LITHOBOLIA.)

YAMA
In Hindu mythology, the judge of the dead.

YANG
In Taoism, the active, masculine and positive cosmic principle that is opposite but always complimentary to yin.

YANG CHING
The Goat God of Chinese mythology and folk belief.

YANSAN
Yoruban god of the winds.

YANTRA
In Hinduism, a mystical diagram drawn on a metal tablet and used in meditation rituals and to invoke divinities.

YARILO
Slavic fertility god and consort of the lunar goddess Marina.

YARROW
A medicinal and culinary herb long associated with the practice of Witchcraft and used in I Ching divinations, love spells, protection spells, exorcisms and rituals to increase psychic powers.

YECH
In Indian folklore, a small, shape-shifting demon who delights in leading travelers astray.

YEGBOGBA
In Dahomean Voodoo, a ring of coiled or twisted iron strands, worn on the second toe of the left foot as a magickal charm against snakebites.

YEHWEZOGBANU
In Dahomean mythology, a dangerous, thirty-horned giant who lives in forests and is a constant threat to hunters.

YEMENJA
Yoruban sea goddess, identified with the siren.

YETI
In folklore, a hirsute, man-like animal with reddish hair that inhabits the snow-covered slopes of the Himalayas; the Abominable Snowman.

YGGDRASIL
In Norse mythology, a sacred ash tree that united Earth, Heaven and the Underworld by its roots and branches.

YIN
In Taoism, the passive, feminine and negative cosmic principle that is opposite but always complimentary to yang.

YOGA
The practice of a special series of physical postures, breathing exercises and meditations to achieve spiritual insight, tranquility and unity of mind and body.

YOGI
A man who practices yoga.

YOGINI
A woman who practices yoga.

YONI
(1) in Tibetan and Indian religion, the sacred symbol of the female principle or female creative energy. (2) the external female genitalia, associated with concepts of the Mother Goddess, the earth, fertility and reproduction.

YULE
One of the four lesser Witches' Sabbats which takes place on the Winter Solstice on or about the 21st of December, originally marking the rebirth of the Sun God from the Earth Goddess. During the Yule Sabbat, Yule logs are burned, mistletoe is hung in doorways and on altars, gifts are exchanged and the Great Horned God who rules the dark half of the year is honored.

YULE LOG
A log ritually burned at Yule to mark the death of winter and the rebirth of the sun. The burning of the Yule log stems from the ancient Pagan custom of the Yule bonfire which was burned to give life and power to the sun, which was thought of as being reborn at the Winter Solstice. In later times, the outdoor bonfire custom was replaced by the indoor burning of logs and red candles etched with carvings of suns and other magickal symbols. As the oak tree was considered to be the Cosmic Tree of the ancient Druids, the Yule log is traditionally oak; however, some Wiccan traditions burn a pine Yule log to symbolize the dying god Attis, Dionysus or Woden. In days of old, the ashes of the Yule log were mixed with cow fodder to aid in symbolic reproduction and was sprinkled over the fields to insure new life and a fertile spring.

ZAKA
In Voodoo, a god of agriculture who appears as a peasant wearing a straw hat, smoking a pipe, and carrying a machete in his hand.

ZAZEN
A form of Zen meditation.

ZENER CARDS
In parapsychology, special cards used in experimental tests for extrasensory perception. The Zener pack consists of 25 cards, five of each of the following symbols: circle, cross, square, star, and a motif consisting of three wavy lines.

ZEUS
The most powerful of the Greek gods, ruler of Heaven and Earth, son of Kronos and Rhea. Zeus is also known as the Cloud-Gatherer, the Lord of Thunderbolts, and the Master of Shape-Shifting. The oak is his sacred tree, the eagle his sacred bird, and gold his sacred color.

ZOANTHROPY
The belief that a man or woman can transform into an animal, acquiring its characteristics.

ZOBOP
In Voodoo, a group of sorcerers, similar to a Witches' coven, who band together for magickal power and strength.

ZODIAC
An invisible circular band in the sky through which the planets are seen to move. It is divided into twelve equal sections called zodiac signs, each 30 degrees wide and bearing the name of a constellation for which it was

originally named but with which it no longer coincides due to the precession of the vernal and autumnal equinoxes. The twelve signs of the zodiac are: Aries the ram, Taurus the bull, Gemini the twins, Cancer the crab, Leo the lion, Virgo the virgin, Libra the balance, Scorpio the scorpion, Sagittarius the archer, Capricorn the goat, Aquarius the water-bearer, and Pisces the fish.

ZODIACAL MAN
In astrology, the concept that different parts of the human anatomy are ruled by the twelve signs of the zodiac: Aries rules the head and brain; Taurus rules the throat and neck; Gemini rules the shoulders, arms and lungs; Cancer rules the chest and stomach; Leo rules the upper back, spine and heart; Virgo rules the intestines and nervous system; Libra rules the lower back and kidneys; Scorpio rules the sex organs; Sagittarius rules the liver, thighs and hips; Capricorn rules the knees, bones, teeth and skin; Aquarius rules the calves, ankles and blood; and Pisces rules the feet and lymph glands.

THE ZOHAR
The Bible of Mysticism first published in the 13th century and believed to be the composition of Rabbi Simon ben Yochai, a second century Jewish luminary renowned as a great mystic. The Zohar deals with nearly every aspect and theme of the occult, and its teachings have exerted a great influence on the Kabbalah as well as all other areas of the occult.

ZOMBIE
In Voodoo folk-legend, a "living" corpse without mind, feeling or will of its own, believed to be reanimated by the occult power of a Voudoun sorcerer-priest and used mainly as a slave.

ZOOMORPHISM
The ability to change from human to animal form (or vice versa) by means of charms, magickal incantations or supernatural powers. The most common forms of zoomorphism are: aeluranthropy (human to cat), boanthropy (human to cow or bull), cynanthropy (human to dog), lepanthropy (human to rabbit or hare), and lycanthropy (human to wolf). Human to animal transformations (as well as animal to human) have been performed since ancient times by sorcerers in nearly every part of the world, especially South America, Africa and Haiti.

ZURVAN
Persian god of time and the father of both Ahura Mazda, the personification of good, and Angra Mainyu, the personification of evil.

ZYA
In black magick and sorcery, a piece of cloth or paper containing the image of a certain man or woman. It is used with evil incantations to bring harm or death to the person it represents.

BIBLIOGRAPHY

Ashley, Leonard: *The Amazing World of Superstition, Prophecy, Luck, Magic and Witchcraft* (Bell, New York, 1988)

Brasch, R.: *Strange Customs* (David McKay Company, New York, 1976)

Brean, Herbert, editor: *The Life Treasury of American Folklore* (Time, Inc., New York, 1961)

Briggs, Katharine: *An Encyclopedia of Fairies, Hobgoblins, Brownies, Bogies and Other Supernatural Creatures* (Pantheon, New York, 1976)

Buckland, Raymond: *Buckland's Complete Book of Witchcraft* (Llewellyn Publications, St. Paul, MN 1986)

Buckland, Raymond: *Witchcraft From the Inside* (Llewellyn Publications, St. Paul, MN 1975) Second Edition.

Budge, E.A. Wallis: *Amulets and Talismans* (University Books, New York, 1961)

Budge, E.A. Wallis: *Egyptian Magic* (Dover, New York, 1971)

Cavendish, Richard: *The Black Arts* (G.P. Putnam's Sons, N.Y. 1967)

Cavendish, Richard, editor: *Man, Myth & Magic* (Marshall Cavendish, New York, 1983)

Cheiro: *Cheiro's Palmistry for All* (Arco Publishing, New York, 1982)

Cirlot, J.E.: *A Dictionary of Symbols* (Philosophical Library, New York, 1971) Second Edition.

Crow, W.B.: *A History of Magic, Witchcraft and Occultism* (Wilshire Books, North Hollywood, California, 1971)

Cunningham, Scott: *The Truth About Witchcraft Today* (Llewellyn Publications, St. Paul, MN 1988)

Cunningham, Scott: *Wicca—A Guide for the Solitary Practitioner* (Llewellyn Publications, St. Paul, MN 1988)

deGivry, Grillot: *Witchcraft, Magic and Alchemy* (Dover, New York, 1971)

Dolphin, Dean: *Rune Magic* (Newcastle Publishing Company, North Hollywood, California 1987)

Drury, Nevill: *Dictionary of Mysticism and the Occult* (Harper and Row, New York, 1985)

Farrar, Janet and Stewart: *A Witche's Bible Compleat* (Magickal Childe, New York, 1984)

Frazer, J.: *The Golden Bough* (MacMillan Company, New York, 1922)

Gibson, Walter B. and Litzka R.: *The Complete Illustrated Book of the Psychic Sciences* (Pocket Books, New York, 1968)

King, Francis: *The Rites of Modern Occult Magic* (MacMillan Company, New York, 1971)

Landsburg, Alan: *In Search of Magic and Witchcraft* (Bantam Books, New York, 1977)

Leach, Maria and Jerome Fried, editors: *Funk and Wagnalls Standard Dictionary of Folklore, Mythology and Legend* (Harper and Row, New York, 1984)

Michelet, J.: *Satanism and Witchcraft* (Arco Publications, London, 1958)

Middleton, John, editor: *Magic, Witchcraft and Curing* (University of Texas Press, Austin, Texas, 1987)

Murray, Alexander S.: *Who's Who in Mythology* (Cresent Books, New York, 1988)

Murray, Margaret A.: *The God of the Witches* (Sampson Low, Marston and Company, Ltd. London, 1931)

Rawcliffe, D.H.: *The Psychology of the Occult* (Derricke Ridgeway Publishing Company, London, 1952)

Robbins, Russell Hope: *The Encyclopedia of Witchcraft and Demonology* (Crown Publishers, New York, 1959)

Scholem, Gershom: *Kabbalah* (Dorset, New York, 1987)

Seligmann, Kurt: *The History of Magic and the Occult* (Pantheon Books, New York, 1948)

Spence, L.: *An Encyclopedia of Occultism* (Routledge and Sons, London, 1920)

Stewart, Louis: *Life Forces* (Andrews and McMeel, New York, 1980)

Summers, Montague: *The History of Witchcraft* (Dorset Press, New York, 1987)

Tallant, R.: *Voodoo in New Orleans* (MacMillan Company, New York, 1945)

Tallman, Marjorie: *Dictionary of American Folklore* (Philosophical Library, New York, 1959)

Trachtenberg, J.: *Jewish Magic and Superstition* (Behrman, New York, 1939)

Valiente, Doreen: *An ABC of Witchcraft Past and Present* (Saint Martin's Press, New York, 1973)

Waite, A.E.: *The Book of Black Magic and of Pacts* (London, 1898)

Waite, A.E.: *A Lexicon of Alchemy* (Samuel Weiser, York Beach, Maine, 1984)

Walker, Barbara G.: *The Women's Encyclopedia of Myths and Secrets* (Harper and Row, New York, 1983)

Wedleck, Harry E.: *Treasury of Witchcraft* (Philosophical Library, New York, 1961)

Wilson, Joyce: *The Complete Book of Palmistry* (Bantam Books, New York, 1971)

Zolar: *Zolar's Encyclopedia of Ancient and Forbidden Knowledge* (Prentice Hall, New York, 1986)

ABOUT THE AUTHOR

GERINA DUNWICH was born on December 27th, 1959 under the sign of Capricorn with a Taurus rising. She is a solitary Witch, cat-lover, poet, professional astrologer and student of the occult arts.

She is the author of *Candlelight Spells, The Magick of Candleburning,* and two books of poetry. She has appeared on numerous radio talk shows across the United States and Canada, and has written many newspaper and magazine articles.

She is a member of the American Biographical Institute Board of Advisors, and is listed in a number of reference works including *Who's Who in the East. Personalities of America,* and *Crossroads: A Who's Who of the Magickal Community.*

Gerina lives near Salem, Massachusetts where she edits and publishes *Golden Isis,* a Wiccan literary journal of mystical poetry and Pagan art.